'There isn't any va
wanted me to stay
taunt me with what
to you in the past. S
of your system!'

At least then she might know, once and for all, what it was all about.

Instead Andreas merely laughed, that soft mirthless laugh that seemed as controlled and calculated as everything else about him. Then with a suddenness that had Magenta's instincts leaping onto red alert, he reached out and caught one end of her scarf. Winding it carefully around his finger, he drew her gently into his dominating sphere.

'Is this a fashion thing?' He tugged lightly at the silk. 'Or is its purpose merely to conceal the remnants of a current lover's carnal appetite?'

'How dare you!' She made to push him away, only to find her hands trapped between his own and the warm hard wall of his chest.

'Yes, I dare,' he growled as his head came down, stopping with his mouth just a breath from hers.

It was the unfathomable dark emotion she saw in his eyes as her trembling gaze wavered beneath his that seemed to rob the breath from her lungs—that and the thunderous hammering of his heart.

She wasn't sure who made the next move, but suddenly their mouths were fused in hungry and antagonized passion and her arms were sliding up around his neck as his stronger ones tightened around her, welding her to him.

Elizabeth Power wanted to be a writer from a very early age, but it wasn't until she was nearly thirty that she took to writing seriously. Writing is now her life. Travelling ranks very highly among her pleasures, and so many places she has visited have been recreated in her books. Living in England's West Country, Elizabeth likes nothing better than taking walks with her husband along the coast or in the adjoining woods, and enjoying all the wonders that nature has to offer.

Recent titles by the same author:

A GREEK ESCAPE
A DELICIOUS DECEPTION
BACK IN THE LION'S DEN
SINS OF THE PAST

VISCONTI'S
FORGOTTEN HEIR

BY
ELIZABETH POWER

First published in Great Britain 2013
by Mills & Boon, an imprint of Harlequin (UK) Limited.
Harlequin (UK) Limited, Eton House, 18-24 Paradise Road,
Richmond, Surrey TW9 1SR

ISBN: 978 0 263 90062 0

Harlequin (UK) policy is to use papers that are natural, renewable
and recyclable products and made from wood grown in sustainable
forests. The logging and manufacturing process conform to the
legal environmental regulations of the country of origin.

Printed and bound in Spain
by Blackprint CPI, Barcelona

VISCONTI'S
FORGOTTEN HEIR

To Alan—for always being there

CHAPTER ONE

As SOON AS she laid eyes on the broad-shouldered man who had just stepped through the door of the crowded wine bar Magenta knew that he was the father of her child.

She didn't suspect, or wonder, or even hope. She simply *knew*.

The stem of the glass she had been wiping suddenly snapped from the tension gripping her fingers, and as she put a steadying hand to her forehead she heard Thomas, her work colleague, enquire, 'Are you all right?'

The laid-back, long-haired college graduate who, like her, was helping out part-time behind the bar until something better came along, was frowning as he came away from the cash register.

She shook her head. Not in answer, but in an attempt to make some sense of the jumble of distant memories that were leaping chaotically through her brain.

Anger. Hostility. Passion. Over all a hungry, all-consuming passion...

Someone spoke to her, trying to give her an order, and she looked up at them with her velvety-brown eyes dazed and her fine features ashen against the darker sheen of her thick swept-up hair.

'Would you mind serving my customer for me?' she appealed croakily to her colleague and, dumping the two pieces

of glass and the tea towel down behind the counter, made a
hasty bid for the merciful seclusion of the Ladies'.

Grabbing the cracked and solitary basin, she struggled to
regain her composure, her lungs dragging in air.

Andreas Visconti. Of *course.* How could she ever have let
anyone persuade her into believing that her child might have
been fathered by anyone else when she'd known in her heart
that she wasn't the type of woman to sleep around, even during those lost and irretrievable months of her life?

She felt sick and stayed where she was, leaning over the
basin, until the nausea subsided, trying to sort out the tangle
of erratic thoughts and images in her mind.

The doctors had told her not to try and force things, and
as the years had passed they had said that the memories she
had lost might never come back. But they were going to. Even
if they were appearing like the distorted shapes of a jigsaw
puzzle she was going to have to piece together. Either way,
right now, she thought, hearing the outer door open and one
of the regular bar staff urgently calling to her, she had to go
back out there and face the music. Even if she didn't know—
or like—the tune that might be playing.

As the countless people in front of him were gradually served,
and a spindly young man finally took his order, at first Andreas Visconti thought he was imagining things when his
gaze drifted to the young woman who was filling glasses
further along the bar.

She was slim, beautiful and flawlessly photogenic, with
her magnificent hair pinned up to emphasise high cheekbones, stunning dark eyes and a lovely mouth above that
long, elegant neck. The vision of her held Andreas in thrall.
As if he was seeing a ghost. Or hallucinating. Both of which
were pretty unlikely, he thought wryly, for a hardened cynic
like himself.

Then someone called her name and he realised that he

wasn't imagining things. It really was her. Magenta James. The girl to whom he had once almost sacrificed his heart— and the whole of his life.

She was looking over her shoulder, listening to something a much older man, whom he guessed was the landlord, was saying, and cruel memory made a hard slash of Andreas's mouth as he caught her tight and rather strained-sounding little laugh.

The last time he had heard that sound was when she had ridiculed his lack of prospects, flaying him with accusations of trying to hold her back from the glittering career she intended to pursue. And now here was Miss High-and-Mighty James pouring drinks in a West Country wine bar! He was, he decided grimly, going to enjoy the next few minutes!

Abandoning the position he had virtually fought to secure, he allowed his curiosity to pull him through the sea of Friday-night revellers which, sensing an unspoken authority, parted effortlessly for him as he shouldered his way along the crowded bar to where she was working.

'Hello, Magenta.'

Beneath her simple black dress—her only concession to colour was the red and black choker she wore around her neck— Magenta's whole body stiffened.

It was inevitable, she thought, her heart racing uncontrollably, that he would notice her. Speak to her. She was unprepared, however, for what his deep, chocolate-rich voice would do to her—or for the impact of his masculinity at close quarters as she turned around from returning a bottle to its shelf at the back of the mirrored bar.

'Andreas...' She could hardly find her voice as she met his unflinching eyes. Sapphire-blue eyes that were a legacy of his mother's English heritage. How easily she had remembered that! she thought, amazed, when her mind was struggling to remember anything else. But those eyes were glittering with

a chilling clarity, and though Magenta strove to recall exactly what it was that had transpired between them she was
certain of nothing beyond the feeling that they had parted on
bad terms. *Very* bad.

'Quite a surprise,' he commented dryly. 'For both of us,
I would imagine.'

Now Magenta recognised a transatlantic lilt in his deep
tones that she somehow knew hadn't been there six years ago,
and with another kick from the darker corners of her mind she
recognised that the healthy bronze of his skin owed as much
to time spent living in the States as to his Anglo-Italian roots.

His well-layered hair was shining like polished jet beneath
the lights, but he looked bigger, broader and tougher than the
young man surfacing from her memory banks. This man was
harder and more forceful. His maturity was reflected in the
span of his wide shoulders, and in that commanding air that
said he had done a lot of living, while his darkly shaded jaw
and the dark hair that was curling above the open neckline
of his casual yet beautifully tailored striped shirt seemed to
scream of his virility.

'I have to admit,' he was saying, oblivious to the turmoil
going on inside her, 'this isn't the sort of place I would have
expected to find you.'

His thinly veiled cynicism stopped her from telling him
that her job there two evenings a week was just one of her
means of being gainfully employed. That she had a day job
as a typist and would shortly be moving on to better things
if the position she had been shortlisted for and was pinning
every last hope on came good during the course of the coming week.

The need to recover those lost months of her life was more
pressing than the need to maintain her self-esteem, so now,
overcoming her fear of what the answer might be, she ventured to ask, 'Wh-where exactly had you expected to find me?'

His mouth jerked down at one side in a gesture of increasing cynicism. 'Is that meant to be some sort of joke?'

The hardness of his eyes made Magenta feel as though she was being touched by cold steel. But, whatever he had expected of her, he wasn't aware that she had lost her memory, was he?

She wanted to tell him but he seemed so hostile, and yet she was trying to make sense of the wildfire he'd ignited in her blood the second she had seen him walk into the bar.

Even the solid barrier of the counter between them couldn't protect her from the images which were bursting from her memory banks. Images of this man kissing her. Undressing her. Of his deep voice whispering sensual phrases that had driven her mindless for him as he'd pleasured and worshipped her body...

She might have forgotten but her body hadn't. This realisation hit her with frightening clarity. And yet the specifics of the bitter conflict that stood so obviously between them continued to elude her memory.

Trying again, she uttered almost involuntarily, 'I don't remember you,' and flinched as her flat little statement produced a sharp, incisive laugh from him.

'You mean you don't *want* to,' he amended with a humourless smile.

I mean I don't. I don't remember what happened.

She put her hand to her forehead, trying to smooth out the chaos of jumbled pieces that were floating up from that part of her brain that remained dormant. In denial.

'You were younger.' She brought her hand down slowly. 'Thinner.' And surely possessing only a fraction of the dynamism of the man who stood before her now?

'Most probably, as I was only twenty-three.'

And working like a slave in your father's restaurant.

Where had *that* come from? Magenta wondered as another recollection kicked in to bring her hand up to her head again.

'Are you all right?'

Through the buzz of conversation she caught an element of concern in the deep, masculine voice.

'Has seeing me again been too much for you? You look a little pale.'

'Well, anyone would compared to you,' she said snappily, realising that he still didn't understand or believe her. 'You look disgustingly healthy.'

'Yes, well…' His hard mouth quirked, tugging in a gesture that was all at once familiar, lazy and disturbingly sensual. 'Life's been good.'

He seemed to need to tell her that, she decided, sifting through the chaff and debris in her mind to try and discover what it was that had brought them from lovers to this hostile place where they now found themselves. But just at that moment her gaze fell to the two tumblers that Thomas had come to put down on the counter in front of them.

A Scotch and soda for Andreas and a bottle of orange juice for…

Trying not to be too obvious, Magenta made a quick survey of the crowded space behind him, catching his mocking expression before she was able to assess who he might have brought with him. She asked quickly, 'Do you come here often?'

Had she really asked him something so trite? So totally banal? she thought, cringing.

'Never.' He was reaching into the pocket of superbly cut grey trousers as Thomas flipped the cap off the orange juice bottle.

'So what brings you here tonight?' Magenta swallowed, wondering why she was dallying with such trivia when all she wanted to do was grab him by the pristine cloth of his shirt and demand that he tell her what had happened between them—except she was afraid of finding out.

Dragging her gaze from the glass that was being filled,

she lifted her velvety-brown eyes to his. A little frisson of awareness shivered through her when she noticed him assessing the slender lines of her body, saw his lips move in a calculated smile.

'Who knows?' he murmured, deeply aware. 'Fate?'

For a moment, from the way he was looking at her and from the husky note he had infused into that beautiful voice of his, the years seemed to fall away and she was nineteen again. Free-spirited. Giddy with hope. *Flighty.* That was what she remembered someone calling her in those days. Yet, whatever faults or failings she might have possessed, she knew now that she had been desperately, terrifyingly besotted with the man before her.

'So what is *this?*' On that rather derogatory note he jerked his chin towards where she stood on the service side of the bar. 'A bit of pin money between assignments? Or didn't the modelling world quite live up to everything you were hoping for?' He tossed a note down on the counter to cover the cost of the drinks.

Of course. Her modelling career. Or lack of it, she thought wryly. Because it had never really taken off.

'Not everything works out the way we plan,' she responded quietly, absently aware of her younger colleague picking up the note before moving away to the till. Thomas was used to customers chatting her up, even if this particular customer had more wow factor than all the others put together.

'Really? So what happened to Rushford? The miracle-maker?'

The deeply intoned words burned with something corrosive, and she wasn't sure whether it was that or the sound of the name that made her suddenly shiver.

'Didn't he live up to your expectations either? And there I was, under the impression you were really going places with that guy.'

With Marcus Rushford? Magenta wanted to laugh out loud.

Instead she was suddenly despairing at how her mind could have let her forget Andreas and yet retained a nightmarish memory of the slick-talking managing agent who had been promoting her for a while.

Confusion swirled around her and she had to take a deep breath to stem the almost physical pain that trying to remember produced.

'Well, as I said...' She gave a little shrug and felt a surge of panic when she realised she had completely forgotten what it was she had been going to say. It still happened sometimes. Times like now, when she felt hot and flummoxed and abnormally stressed. 'Not...' Mercifully the words flooded back, even though she stumbled over them in attempting to get them out. 'Not...everything goes to plan.'

'Evidently not.' He glanced towards where Thomas was waiting behind the middle-aged man who clearly paid their wages, who was sorting out some problem with the cash machine.

Magenta wished he would hurry up. It was purgatory standing there talking to a man who so clearly resented her when her screaming senses were taunting her with the knowledge of how his skin had felt beneath her fingers and how he had shown her pleasure such as her untutored body had never known. If it *had* been untutored, she thought. As far as she knew she could have been as free with her favours as her mother had led her to believe. She had no recollection of those lost months of her life, but her torpid brain had always rejected that thought as repugnant and totally alien to her.

'So what happened to the career? Did Rushford fail to deliver on his promises? Or is that just a rumour? Like the way he cut loose because he couldn't face the responsibility of fatherhood?'

The fact that this man knew she had been expecting a baby sent Magenta's thoughts spinning in a vortex of confusion.

Her hand went to her forehead. Noticing the way it trembled, she brought it quickly down again.

'I'm sorry,' he said, sounding anything but. 'Is that still a sore point?'

His sarcasm dug deep, but she was too busy trying to stay upright to ask him why he believed Theo was Marcus Rushford's child.

Gripping the edge of the bar with both hands for support, and dragging in lungfuls of much-needed air, she murmured, 'I'd prefer not to discuss my son, if it's…all the same to you.' Had he detected that awkwardness—that lack of fluency in her speech which it had taken her a long time to overcome? 'Not here. Not over a bar.'

Not anywhere, she resolved silently. *Not until I know what happened. What it was I did to make you despise me, as you clearly do.*

His black hair gleamed as he dipped his head in acknowledgement. 'I can't help admitting I'm surprised that the girl I knew would let a little thing like motherhood stand in the way of her plans.'

That didn't sound like her at all, Magenta thought, puzzled. She loved little Theo more than anything else in this world. He was the moon and the stars and the earth to her, she mused with a wistful little smile, and she loved him so much it hurt.

Tentatively, resting her arm on the counter and supporting her chin with her hand, she invited, 'So, tell me about the girl you knew.'

He laughed softly and leaned forward so that she caught the shiver of his breath against her hair, the subtle and yet disturbing sensuality of his personal masculine scent. 'I really don't think you'd welcome hearing it,' he murmured silkily.

The glittering blue of his eyes touched on her upturned mouth. A mouth more than one photographer had complimented, saying it had a natural pout.

Quickly Magenta drew back, standing tall again now that the swaying sensation of a few moments ago had passed.

'Maybe you're getting me mixed up with someone else,' she ventured, hoping against hope that it might be true, but knowing in her heart of hearts that it wasn't. The way her mind and her body had reacted the moment she'd seen him come through that door dispelled any doubt that they had been lovers. 'Or maybe you just didn't know me very well.'

'Oh, I think I did.'

His tone, though soft, held a wealth of derogatory meaning, and Magenta wished someone else would grab her attention—demand to be served. But no one did. He obviously commanded too much respect for anyone to challenge him over monopolising one of the bar staff, and secretly she wondered what he did for a living. What it was that gave him his unmistakable air of autonomy—that bred-in-the-bone confidence? Because he hadn't got that from working all hours in a backstreet Italian restaurant, and from the flashes of hazy memory that were puncturing her brain that was the situation in which she was putting him.

'Well, as I said, I don't remember.' She would hate to admit it to this man who was being so openly hostile, and yet she was on the verge of telling him why, in the hope that he would be able to break down some of the barriers in her brain, when he let out a sound of increasing impatience.

'You're still trying to deny we even *knew* each other?'

He sounded so hard and looked so forbidding that Magenta felt her confidence waning, felt herself shrinking back behind the curtain of self-protection she'd created in order to hide from life until she was ready to grit her teeth and allow herself to take on new challenges—challenges which at the start had seemed insurmountable. But, determined not to let this man's prejudice undo all the good that the past few years of hard work and perseverance had produced, she swallowed her fears and misgivings and plunged in.

'What did I do? Stop seeing you because of someone else? Or was it my career? Whatever it was, at least you can go away with the satisfaction of knowing that I probably got my just deserts and didn't realise all those dreams I was obviously stupid enough to throw you over for.'

His lips held a ruminative smile that did nothing to warm the icy blue of his eyes.

'Now, there you're wrong,' he murmured in a voice that was silkily soft. 'Our little...interlude wasn't significant enough for me to harbour any long-term desire for revenge, so there's no need to beat yourself up over it unnecessarily, Magenta.' His tone suggested that that was the last thing he expected her to be doing. 'We're all guilty at times—especially when we're young—of setting our sights beyond what we can realistically achieve.'

He'd said he wasn't harbouring any desire for revenge over whatever she was supposed to have done, but it was obvious to Magenta that he was getting satisfaction from seeing her now.

'You'd be surprised what I've *achieved* over the past five years or so.' Her pride forced her to utter the words before she could control the urge.

'Oh, really?' A quizzical eyebrow lifted. 'Like what?'

Like learning to walk again. Like holding a knife and fork! Like taking over responsibility for my own precious little baby. Like staying alive!

Unconsciously she fingered the red and black choker that lay strategically over one of her now fading scars. He didn't need to know any of that. Or about the Business Studies course she had taken, which had enabled her to apply for the new position she was hoping to get, which would lift her out of temping by day and working behind a bar a couple of nights a week and allow her to provide a better future for her and her son.

'It isn't important,' she dismissed on a defeated little note. Anyway, he was acknowledging lanky young Thomas, who had loped back with his change and was apologising for keeping him waiting.

Magenta's gaze fell to the lean, masculine hands now lifting the tumblers off the counter. Hands which she knew had once taken her to paradise and back and which were surprisingly devoid of any rings.

But there *were* two glasses. Two drinks...

His eyes caught her unconcealed interest and he shifted his position slightly—deliberately, Magenta guessed—creating a breach in the crowd and allowing her eyes to make their way to the smartly dressed, very attractive redhead sitting at one of the tables. She was looking at Andreas with a smile born of familiarity and undisguised appreciation.

Looking quickly back at Andreas, Magenta felt his eyes resting too intently on her face. Eyes that were penetratingly perceptive. Much too aware...

'As I said...' His mouth twisted with cruel satisfaction. 'Life's been good,' he reiterated, before moving away.

Magenta stood there for a moment, feeling as though she had just come through some invisible, indescribable battle. She felt sick, and her head was thumping, and all she wanted to do was run away and hide. But someone had started giving her an order and she knew she couldn't just run off without doing her job, even if it *was* under the smug gaze of a man who clearly despised her.

'Is that guy a boyfriend of yours?' Thomas asked over his shoulder as Magenta finished serving the woman.

Over the sounds of a live band setting up their instruments in the designated corner of the wine bar, she could only manage a negative murmur as she shook her head.

'No?' A mousy eyebrow disappeared beneath a tangled mass of equally mousy hair. 'Then why was he looking at you as though he was determined to rip that dress off?'

'Don't be silly.' Dazed though she was, her colleague's observation pumped up Magenta's skittering heart-rate, lend-ing a pink tinge to her otherwise colour-leeched face. 'He's with someone.'

'He was.'

'What?' She couldn't see past the wall of customers and the band doing its sound check against a babble of laughter and mixed conversation.

'I swear he downed that whisky in one and hustled his girlfriend out the door before she had time to draw breath.'

For some reason Magenta's stomach seemed to turn over. 'He did?' Another glimpse towards his table through a sudden gap in the human wall showed only an empty tumbler and a barely touched glass of orange juice that had clearly been hastily abandoned.

'So? They must have been in a hurry to get somewhere,' Magenta supplied, wondering why they had left in such a rush. Was it because of her? she speculated, her heart hammering against her ribcage and her head starting to swim. Couldn't he stand being under the same roof with her long enough for the woman he'd brought with him even to finish her drink?

'Hey! Are you all right?' she heard Thomas ask again as she staggered, dropping her head into her hands to try and stanch the rising nausea.

'No, I'm sorry. Could you call me a taxi?' she appealed to Thomas, before staggering to the Ladies' again, where she was violently sick.

He had behaved badly, Andreas thought as he was driving home alone, but it had been both shocking and unsettling—far more unsettling than he wanted to admit—seeing Magenta again.

He had been twenty-three to her nineteen, and just a dogsbody in his father's floundering business, and yet he should have known right away what kind of a girl she was. She had been living in a rundown terraced house with her man-crazy alcoholic mother, who hadn't even known who Magenta's father was!

He'd taken pity on her, Andreas told himself, as the beam of oncoming headlamps slashed cold light across his hardening features. Why else would he have got himself mixed up with her? But hot on the heels of that self-deluded question came the real answer—one that heated his veins and caused a heavy throbbing in his blood.

Because she'd been warm and exciting and more beautiful than any other girl he had ever met in his life—and he had known quite a few, even then. Although not enough to have learned that girls like Magenta James were only out for one thing. A good time—regardless of the cost to anyone else, particularly the poor sucker who happened to be providing her with that good time!

Tension locked his jaw as he turned the steering wheel to cross a junction.

She had known she was beautiful. That was the problem. A part-time receptionist who had been on every model agency's books, following every lead and promotion she could grasp in a bid to capitalise on her beauty. That was when she hadn't been at home, trying to shake her mother out of a drunken stupor!

They had become lovers almost at once, just a few days after they'd started dating, and only a week after he had seen her in his father's restaurant with a group of women during a lively hen party. Surprisingly, she had been a virgin the first time he had made love to her, and yet he had unleashed a fire in her that he'd been foolish enough to believe burned for him alone.

They had made love everywhere. In his van. In the flat above the restaurant when his father and grandmother were out. In her surprisingly immaculate, sparsely furnished little bedroom which had seemed like an oasis amidst the clutter

and chaos of her mother's damp and crumbling, sadly ne-
glected Edwardian house.

It hadn't mattered one iota that his family hadn't liked
her—although he had wondered, with the gentle memory
of his mother, how she might have viewed Magenta if she
hadn't died while he was still very young. His grandmother,
though, had been totally out of touch with people of his gen-
eration, and his father...

He slammed his mind shut as a well of excruciating pain
and reproach threatened to invade it. Their disapproval, he
remembered, had only intensified the excitement of being
with her.

Of course they had known what she was like; they had
been able to see through the thin veil of her bewitching beauty
when he hadn't. He had been blinded and totally duped by
her impassioned but hollow declarations of love.

He had been hardworking, loyal to his father, and yet ambitious. And he had at least been able to see and recognise the
flaws in the way in which his father had run the restaurant.
Giuseppe Visconti had been a far more proficient chef than
he had been a businessman, and as proud an Italian as he'd
been a dictator of a father, and he had refused to listen to his
son's radical plans for saving and developing the business.

'Over my dead body.'

Andreas still flinched now from recalling his father's exact
words.

'You will never have a foothold in this business. *Dio mio!*
Never! Not while you are stupid enough to be mixed up with
that girl.'

He had been a blind and naive fool to believe that love
could conquer all, that with Magenta James beside him he
could overcome his family's prejudices and his father's stub-
bornness. What he hadn't realised, he reflected coldly, was
that the lovely Magenta had only been amusing herself in his
bed—that even as he had been drowning in the heat of their

mutual passion she had already been sexually entangled with someone else.

He hadn't wanted to believe his father's smug revelations—and wouldn't have if he hadn't gone round to her house unexpectedly and seen Rushford's car parked outside. A huge and expensive black saloon that had stood out like a sore thumb in her rather downmarket neighbourhood, and especially outside her mother's particularly rundown house.

He'd driven away on that occasion, still unable to believe his eyes—and indeed what his family had been telling him. But hadn't he had graphic proof of her infidelity himself?

'Do you really think I was ever serious about you? About *this*?' she had scoffed on an almost hysterical little bubble of laughter the last time he had seen her.

She'd shot a disparaging glance around the deserted and already failing restaurant. That was when she had informed him of all her precious Svengali was doing for her and all that she was intending to achieve.

He had had a row with Giuseppe Visconti that night. One of many, he reflected. But this one had been different. It had been the squaring up of two male animals intent only on victory over the other. Savage. Almost coming to blows. He'd blamed his father for the outcome of his relationship with Magenta. Giuseppe had called her names, foul names that Andreas had never been able to repeat, and he'd accused his father of being jealous of his youth and his prospects, of depriving him of his right to be his own man.

His father had died in his arms that night after the angry tirade that had been too much for his unexpectedly weak heart to take. Two months later his grandmother had put the restaurant on the market to pay off the loans the business had been unable to meet, determined to go back to her native Italy.

Some time afterwards, when Andreas had been in America, someone—he couldn't remember who—had told him that Magenta was living in the lap of luxury with a big-shot called Marcus Rushford and that she was expecting his baby.

Yes, he'd behaved badly tonight, Andreas reflected grimly as he swung his car through the electrically operated gates of his Surrey mansion. But at the end of it, looking back, he decided that he hadn't behaved badly *enough!*

CHAPTER TWO

ALL THE WAY home in the taxi Magenta's head was throbbing, pulsating with an invasion of jumbled images. When at last she had paid the driver, was staggering towards the privacy of her own bathroom, the kaleidoscope of confusing images started to take some form.

Meeting Andreas in that restaurant. Laughing with Andreas. Making love with him.... Where, it didn't matter. It hadn't mattered then. She pressed the heels of her hands against the wells of her eyes, her breath catching as a heated and desperate desire took hold in her mind. Why had it been desperate? She shook her head to try and jolt herself into remembering. She *had* to remember...

There was a big man. Sullen. Andreas's father! And Maria. Maria was his grandmother! Oh, but there had been such ill feeling! She recalled feeling the lowest of the low. There was shouting now. Andreas was shouting at *her*. Telling her she was shallow-minded and materialistic. Telling her she was no good—just like her mother.

In a crumpled heap beside the toilet she relieved herself of the nausea that remembering produced and wiped her mouth with the back of her hand. For the first time she was glad that Theo was spending part of his school holiday in the country with her great-aunt. It would have distressed her little boy to have seen her in such a state.

Winding her arms around herself, she ached for him, missing him as much as on the day when she had woken up from that coma to realise she'd lost not only two months of her life, but also the baby she'd remembered carrying. It was the only thing she *had* remembered. Except that she hadn't lost him...

She started sobbing with all the same poignancy with which she'd sobbed that day when her widowed aunt, Josie Ashton, had brought her healthy eight-week-old son into the hospital and laid him against her breast. Dear Great-Aunt Josie, with her abrupt manner and her outspokenness, whom Magenta hadn't seen for at least ten years. But the woman had had no qualms, she remembered, about answering her mother's cry for help when a sick daughter and the arrival of a new grandson had been too much for Jeanette James to cope with.

She was sobbing equally, though, for the way her mind had blanked out her child's father. How could she have forgotten him? she agonised, feeling the loss for her son, for the lack of a father figure in his life, rather than for herself. What had he done that had driven her subconscious into shut down so completely? What had *she* done? she wondered, suddenly seized by the frightening possibility that she might somehow *deserve* his condemnation.

For heaven's sake, *think!* she urged herself, desperate for answers.

But the floodgates that had started to open refused to budge any further, and by the time she arrived at her interview the following week, she felt worn out from the effort of trying to force them apart.

'I see from your CV that you only acquired your qualification in Business Studies over the last eighteen months, and that you didn't work anywhere on a permanent basis for the preceding four years,' said the older of the two women who were interviewing her.

There was a middle-aged man there too, who suddenly

chipped in with, 'May I ask what you were doing in the meantime?'

'I've been bringing up my son,' Magenta supplied, relieved to be able to say it without any hesitation in her speech, especially when she felt as though she were facing an inquisition.

The interview was for the post of PA to the marketing manager of a rapidly expanding hotel chain, and Magenta had gone for a totally sophisticated image. With her hair up, and wearing a tailored grey suit and maroon camisole, with the stripes in the silk scarf around her neck blending the two colours, she didn't think she could have looked smarter if she had tried.

She was desperate to get this job to help her pay off her mounting debts so that she could stay on in her flat and give her child all the security and comforts she herself had never had. For that reason she had chosen not to disclose everything about herself when she had applied for this position three weeks ago, certain that the reason she hadn't been offered any of the endless list of the other jobs she had applied for was because she had been too forthcoming with the truth.

But this job looked as if it was hers—particularly as the older woman on the other side of the desk was making no secret of the fact that she favoured Magenta over the only other candidate on the shortlist.

'And you won't find it a problem dividing your time between the demands of the office and those of a five-year-old?' The younger, fair-haired woman, by the name of Lana Barleythorne, was challenging her. 'He can't have been at school very long...'

'Well over a year,' Magenta supplied, proud of how bright and advanced for his age her little boy was. 'And I do have very satisfactory childcare.' She didn't tell them about Great-Aunt Josie, who had shown her and Theo such unconditional love when they had needed it most.

Her answer seemed to please her interviewers, because

the more matronly of the two women was now explaining that the marketing manager for whom she'd be working was attending a conference that day but had asked if Magenta would be prepared to come in and meet her later in the week.

Yes! Had she been on her own Magenta would have punched the air in triumph. 'Of course,' she answered calmly instead, hoping she didn't look too desperately relieved.

She was still trying to keep her concentration on what they were saying, and to stop herself grinning from ear to ear, when a knock had her gaze swivelling across the large modern office to the tall man in an immaculate dark suit who was striding in.

Andreas! Magenta tried to force his name past her lips but no sound came out.

What was he doing here? she wondered, aghast. And why had he barged in dressed like that, as though he had every right to?

'Mr Visconti…' The older woman, looking surprised, was getting to her feet, but a silent command from him had her subsiding back onto her chair. 'This is Miss James,' she explained. 'We were just about to wind up her interview.'

'I know.'

The deep voice was calm. Matter-of-fact. But he hadn't yet looked her way and Magenta guessed that he hadn't connected the name with her or realised that it was his ex the woman was referring to, now sitting there in a state of shock.

'That's why I came in.'

The impact of his sudden entrance had made her go weak all over, she realised, and then he suddenly glanced her way and his intensely blue eyes met the stunned velvety-brown of hers.

'Mr Visconti is our Chief Executive,' her principal interviewer was telling Magenta, through what seemed like a thick and muffling fog.

Chief Executive? How could he be? she wondered when she finally managed to grasp what the woman had said.

'He's the man we're all ultimately answerable to,' said Lana Barleythorne, who seemed to be having difficulty keeping her eyes off him. 'He has the last word on whatever changes might be taking place throughout the chain.'

'And I'm afraid this position has already been filled.'

He took his eyes off Magenta only briefly, to direct a glance towards the people she now realised, staggeringly, were his employees.

'But we thought—' piped up Lara, his clearly adoring fan.

'It's Miss Nicholls—the last candidate,' he stated tonelessly, and in a way that imparted to anyone who might dare to challenge him that his decision was final and no one else had the authority to question it. 'I've already spoken to...'

Numbly, Magenta only half heard him saying that he had spoken to his marketing manager and she was happy to take the other candidate on.

'I see.' The woman who was obviously the spokesperson for the three sounded surprised.

And all at once, through her shock and mounting dismay over losing a job that had not only been within her grasp but which she had been counting on to get her out of financial deep water, Magenta began to see things as they really were.

He had known she was in here. Probably from some list he had vetted before coming in. Which was why he hadn't shown any sign of surprise or shock when he had seen her. Because he had already decided—even before he had opened that door—to snatch the chance of that job right out of her hands!

'Miss James...'

The woman Magenta knew she had won over from the start made a futile little gesture with her hands.

'What can I say? Except that I think we owe you an apology.'

For what? Magenta thought, hurting, angry. For building

up her hopes? For making her think she could be out of the woods with her finances and her barely affordable flat? For throwing her back into the never-ending queue for far too few realistically paid jobs? Perhaps they didn't have bills to pay and debts to settle, but she did! And now, just because she'd walked into a company controlled by this man with an obvious score to settle, none of those bills were ever likely to be paid!

Not caring any more about what impression she created, she leaped up from her chair and, in response to the woman's suggestion about owing her an apology, uttered, 'Yes, I believe you do! I've had to take a whole morning off work—without pay—to enable me to come to this interview today, and I think that the least you could have done in return would have been to get your facts straight! It might not be any skin off *your* noses to drag people here under false pretences, but if this is the way your company operates then I hope your paying customers don't arrive at their hotels only to find the previous guests still occupying their beds!'

She felt sorry for her interviewers—particularly the woman who had shown such enthusiasm for her capabilities before their cold and calculating boss had walked in. Her venom was directed solely at Andreas. She hadn't wanted to show him up in front of his staff, but if she had, she thought fiercely, then after what he had just done it was no more than he deserved!

'That's all I have to say,' she concluded. And she had done so without embarrassing herself, or even tripping over her words, she realised, pivoting away from them—from *him*—as the ordeal and the thought of what it would mean for her and Theo brought shaming tears to her eyes.

'Miss James.'

The deep, masculine voice addressed her formally from across the room but she ignored it, tearing over the high-

polished floor to the door through which she had come with
such high hopes only half an hour earlier.

'Magenta!'

He didn't seem bothered by what the others might make of
him calling her by her first name, and images of a young man
swam before her eyes. A young man who was determined,
high-spirited and unrestrained—a young Andreas who refused to be dominated by his father's will....

His softer command—and it *had* been a command, though
infused with a persuasive familiarity—stopped her in her
tracks.

Standing there, with her heart banging against her ribcage,
she brought her head up, breathing deeply to control her humiliating emotion, squaring her back beneath the silver-grey
jacket before she steeled herself to turn around.

'There is another vacancy,' Andreas said.

The distance she had put between them had given him a
greater vantage point from which to study her, and he was
doing just that, allowing his cool gaze to travel over the slender lines of her body in a way that made Magenta almost forget that there were other people in the room.

She looked at him questioningly but he was addressing
the other three, who appeared to be silently querying his
declaration.

'It's all right. I'll handle this,' Andreas told them, and one
by one they filed out—the younger woman seeming to shoot
daggers in Magenta's direction, the elder sending her a surprisingly knowing smile.

'So what is the vacancy?' Magenta's mouth felt dry as the
door closed behind them. The air seemed charged with something sensual, stiflingly intimate even in the spacious modern
office. 'Or is this all a clever ploy to try and keep me here?'

Andreas moved around the desk and leaned back against
it, his hands clutching his elbows, one foot crossed over the
other.

'I think we should talk first,' he said.

'What about? Why you just ruined my chances of getting a job I was counting on?' Tremblingly, because she was almost afraid of knowing the answer, she tagged on, 'What did I ever do to you that you should dislike me so much?'

He laughed very softly, but there was no humour in his eyes. 'Come and sit down,' he ordered with a jerk of his chin towards her vacated chair.

'I prefer to stand, if you don't mind.'

She did, however, move closer to him—close enough to bring her hands down on the back of the chair for some much-needed support.

'As you wish.' This was accompanied by a gesture of one long, lean hand.

'Tell me what I did. I told you—I'm having difficulty remembering.'

'That's convenient.'

'It's the truth.'

'And from experience we both know that you can be remarkably sparing with *that*.'

His tone flayed, bringing Magenta's lashes down like lustrous ebony against the pale translucency of her skin.

'We dated...' She came around the chair and like an automaton, despite what she had said, sat down upon it, starkly aware of the cynical sound her comment produced.

'Well, that's one up on what you claimed to know last Friday,' he remarked. 'But if *my* memory serves me correctly we did a whole lot more than that.'

Images invaded of ripping clothes and devouring kisses. Of tangled limbs and naked bodies. Of herself spread-eagled on a bed in glorious abandon to this man's driving passion.

She shook her head and realised that he had relinquished his position on the desk.

'You're crying,' he observed, coming towards her and noting the emotion still moistening her eyes after losing the job she'd struggled so long and hard for. 'It always heightened my pleasure to kiss you after you had been crying. It made your mouth so inviting. So unbelievably soft...'

His voice had grown quieter, Magenta realised, tormented again by sensual images of the two of them together, by the arousing sensations that were invading every erogenous zone in her body.

'I'm not crying,' she bluffed, in rejection of everything he was saying—and then caught a sudden, startling glimpse of herself from somewhere in her past, crying bitterly. She was sobbing because she had to leave him. She'd known she had to get away from him. But *why?* 'I'm annoyed—angry—humiliated. But I'm certainly not crying. If you want to hurt me then that's your problem—not mine. But, just for the record, was that rather uncalled-for remark a roundabout way of saying that *you* were always upsetting *me?*'

Within the hard framework of his features his devastating mouth turned uncompromisingly grim. 'I wasn't the one responsible for causing you pain in the past, and I certainly did nothing to make you weep. Except in bed.'

His continual references to the passion they had shared were unsettling her beyond belief. As he probably intended them to, she realised, catching a different sound now from the darkest corners of her mind. The sound of herself sobbing with desire at the enslaving, unparalleled pleasure he was giving her. But there were other things too. Things she didn't want to remember, which his disturbing presence alone was bringing back to her.

'Your family hated me.'

'That was my family.'

'Especially your father.'

His face took on the cast of an impregnable steel mask. 'And with good cause, I think. In the end.'

She wanted to ask him why. What it was she had done to make him despise her so much. But he was still too cold, too distant and far too unapproachable. And anyway she was afraid of what hearing the truth might do to her.

'How is he? Your father?' she enquired tentatively.

'My father's dead.'

From the way he said it he might easily be implying that *she* had had something to do with it. Oh, no! She couldn't have, surely? she thought, shuddering at the hard, cold emotion she saw in his eyes which seemed to be piercing her like shards of ice.

'He's dead,' he reiterated. 'As you would have known if you hadn't been so tied up with making a name for yourself.'

'Oh, I had a *name,* Andreas.' It rushed back at her, hurtful and destructive. 'And it wasn't very complimentary. But I suppose you think I deserved what your grandmother called me?'

Her voice was low and controlled. She was determined not to let him see her trembling. And it wasn't just the remembered pain of that time that was ripping through her memory banks and slashing at her now with such wounding cruelty, but the cold way she had just been informed that Giuseppe Visconti had died.

She wanted to ask Andreas what had happened but was even too cowardly to do that. Instead she dropped her head into her hands and groaned as a sudden vision flashed before her eyes.

It was of plate glass and fluorescent lighting where once there had been red and white chequered curtains and candlelit windows; an internet café where the little restaurant had been. She had found herself standing outside it once a couple of years ago, not even realising why, or what she was doing there. She only remembered that the experience had chilled her to the bone.

Watching her, Andreas frowned—and then reminded himself what a good actress she was.

'I'm afraid I'm not really taken in by this display of crocodile tears,' he said bluntly, but as she lifted her head and dragged her fingers down her face the dark smudges under her eyes and her pallor shocked him. 'Are you all right?' he asked, concerned.

'I'm fine.'

'No, you're not. I think you'd better come with me.' He was urging her up from her chair before she had time to think.

'Where are we going?' she asked weakly as he bundled her into a waiting lift in the lobby.

'As I said, we have to talk,' he said, setting the lift in motion.

Released now from the pressure of his hand at her elbow, but finding his whole persona too disturbing in such a confined space, Magenta stepped as far away from him as she could.

A faint smile touched the firm, masculine mouth, as though he knew exactly why she had done that.

'And, as *I* said, what about?' She could feel the blood returning to her face and was managing to gather her wits about her again. 'There isn't any other vacancy, is there? You just wanted me to stay behind so that you could taunt me with whatever it is you think I did to you in the past. So go ahead. Get it all out of your system!'

At least then she might know, once and for all, what it was all about.

Instead he merely laughed, and that soft, mirthless laugh seemed as controlled and calculated as everything else about him. Then, with a suddenness that had Magenta's instincts leaping onto red alert, he reached out and caught one end of her scarf. Winding it carefully around his finger, he drew her gently into his dominating sphere.

'Is this a fashion thing?' He tugged lightly at the silk. 'Or is its purpose merely to conceal the remnants of your current lover's carnal appetite?'

'How dare you?' She made to push him away, only to find

her hands trapped between his own and the warm hard wall of his chest.

'Yes, I dare,' he growled, and his head came down, stopping with his mouth just a breath from hers.

It was the unfathomable dark emotion she saw in his eyes as her trembling gaze wavered beneath his that seemed to rob the breath from her lungs—that and the thunderous hammering of his heart.

She wasn't sure who made the next move, but suddenly their mouths were fused in a hungry and antagonistic passion, and her arms were sliding up around his neck as his stronger ones tightened around her, welding her to him.

She was nineteen again and she was laughing with him, her heart on fire, wild with a new sense of freedom and excitement. But he wasn't laughing with her. She was laughing all by herself. And she was being weighed down with such a feeling of remorse and shame.

Fighting Andreas, she was surprised when he let her go— and so roughly that she almost stumbled back against the far wall of the lift.

Groaning, she put her hand to her mouth, stemming a new bout of nausea. She realised it wasn't that devastating kiss that was responsible for her crushing feeling of self-disgust.

'Forgive me for being under the impression that you wanted that as much as I did. Even when you were sleeping with another man you were never averse to my touch.'

Whether she deserved that or not, Magenta felt her hand itch to make contact with his dark, judgmental face.

'Don't even think about it,' he advised, breathing as erratically as she was.

She was grateful when the lift opened, and didn't need Andreas's prompting to step out.

'Where are we?' she demanded over her shoulder. Before he answered she realised that they were on the top floor of the building, where wide windows gave a breathtaking view of the bustling capital below.

'You aren't feeling well,' Andreas commented as he moved past her and used a security key to open the door to an executive suite. 'Whether from fatigue or simply—as your weight seems to suggest—because you aren't eating enough, I didn't welcome the thought of you passing out on me down there.'

'Thanks,' Magenta responded tartly, her breathing still irregular from the unexpected and disturbing scenario in the lift. Or *had* she expected it? The question raged through her consciousness with the disturbance of a ten-force gale. She only knew she had wanted it. Dear heaven, had she wanted it!

A low whistle passed through her lips as Andreas let her into a luxuriously decorated office. It was all there: the solid wood floor, an imposing mahogany desk that looked out over the city, the softest leather settees, luscious plants and huge windows to complete his commercial kingdom.

'What did you do? Win the lottery or something?' Vague as her memories were, Magenta couldn't equate how the son of a humble restaurateur could have gone from a virtual dogsbody in his father's restaurant to CEO of a chain of exclusive hotels.

'You know I never leave anything to chance.'

Fat chance. His declaration brought those two words to the forefront of her mind. It seemed to be something she had said once in connection with his telling her what he intended to do with his life.

'I think you should have a brandy,' he advised, already on his way over to a cabinet on the far side of the room.

'I never drink.' If there were still facts missing from her life then that was one fact she had never allowed herself to forget. 'I've seen what it can do to people.'

He nodded, knowing what had prompted her to say it. Her mother.

Magenta recalled how hard she had battled as a teenager

against her mother's addiction, which had been constantly fuelled by a string of broken relationships.

'In that case I'll send for some coffee.' Andreas picked up the phone and ordered some to be brought up in that deep, authoritative voice of his. 'Sit down,' he invited.

Magenta stood there, thinking of the young man whose hands she had been so drawn to when he'd set that first cup of coffee he had made down in front of her. She couldn't get over how this new present-day Andreas didn't even have to perform *that* simple task himself.

'So what happened, Andreas?' she asked, still standing her ground. 'I know you're dying to tell me, otherwise you wouldn't have brought me up here.' Unless, of course, he had it in his mind to take up where they had left off in the lift, she thought, her mind rejecting the idea as strongly as her body was responding to it, just to mock her.

'You're perfectly safe—if you're thinking what I think you are,' that masculine voice intoned, startling her into obeying his silent command to sink down onto one of the huge and plushly inviting settees. 'I don't intend to make overtures to a woman who showed such repugnance at my kisses. You put on a good show of displaying that out there—even if we both know that that's really all it was. A *show*,' he emphasised.

He was entirely miscalculating the reason for her shattering reaction in the lift—something she was certain he didn't do very often.

'I had a lucky break when an uncle I never knew died and left me three restaurants between Naples and Milan.'

'So you *do* believe in luck?' she uttered, reminding him of what he'd said a few moments ago about never leaving anything to chance.

'If one can expand on that luck and make things happen.'

'Which you did, of course.'

'It was a gruelling, round-the-clock enterprise, building up those restaurants and then opening more in the States, where

I was living until less than a year ago, then investing in and turning around the fortunes of a series of small hotels. That led on to bigger things that finally brought me here. Nothing is impossible if you're prepared to work hard enough.'

That judgmental note was back in his voice again, and unthinkingly she uttered, 'Instead of trading on one's physical attributes like you seem to want to accuse me of doing?'

He gave her a withering look but didn't actually comment as he crossed the room and came and stood in front of her. 'Tell me about your son,' he said without any preamble. 'It can't be any picnic, bringing up a child on your own.'

His words triggered something that was too elusive to grasp, yet what lingered in the forefront of her mind was a real and crushing fear. An intangible yet instinctive knowledge that if this man realised she'd had his child he wouldn't hesitate to try and take Theo away from her....

'What...what do you want to know?' she faltered, casting her eyes down briefly, her lashes dark wings of ebony against the wells of her eyes. Had he detected the tension in her? she wondered when she saw the deepening groove between his thick black brows. Guessed at the reasons for her reluctance to discuss her little boy?

'Did Rushford really dump you before you'd even reached the full term of your pregnancy?'

So he was still insisting that Marcus Rushford had been her lover. The thought of sleeping with her former exploitative agent made her stomach queasy, even though he was an attractive and very worldly man. That was preferable, though, to the possible consequences of explaining to Andreas that *he* was the father of her child, and crazily she uttered, 'If it makes you feel smug, believe it.'

His response to that was merely a slight twitching of his mouth. 'So...does Rushford even see his son?'

Magenta's mouth felt dry. She wished the coffee would

come as she struggled for composure under this very disturbing line of questioning.

'His name is Marcus. And, no, he doesn't ever see Theo.'

'What?' Hard lines of disbelief lined Andreas's face. 'Never?' He looked and sounded appalled.

'Never,' she uttered dismissively, deciding to end the conversation there and then. 'There never was another vacancy, was there?' she accused again, deciding he really *had* only brought her up here to satisfy some warped agenda of his own. 'So now you've shown me just how well you're doing...' quickly she got to her feet '...and clarified that all those rumours you heard about me were probably true, I'll be on my way.'

Trying to save face before she walked away from him, wondering how in the world she was ever going to pay her mounting bills, she forced back her concerns and told him, 'This wasn't the only job I was being interviewed for today.'

She hadn't even reached the door when she heard him say confidently, 'Liar.'

She swung round, speechless at his mocking arrogance.

'I haven't got where I am today without gaining some insight into human nature,' he disclosed, moving towards her with the self-possessed demeanour of a man who knew he was right. 'A woman doesn't normally go to pieces over losing the prospect of a job, as you nearly did down there, if she has another package tucked neatly up her sleeve and hasn't pinned her hopes on just one that she thinks might be a little way out of her league.'

Was that what he thought? That she wasn't suitable for the post? 'I didn't think any such thing! And I wasn't going to pieces, as you'd like to imagine I was.'

'Weren't you?' The trace of a smile played around his mouth. 'You seem to forget—I know you. Although you've done your level best since we met again last Friday to try and make me believe you're suffering from some sort of selective memory loss, I *do* know you, Magenta. Very well. I know how your eyes always glitter when you're inviting me to challenge you. How the excitement of some delightful reprisal serves to put colour in your cheeks.'

He was moving purposefully towards her, making her instincts scream in rejection. Her body, though, trembled with the excitement he had spoken of—even as she feared that he might just remind her of what other responses he could evoke in her, as he had done on the way up here.

'Apart from which,' he added, coming to a stop just centimetres in front of her, 'you were almost visibly shaking. Just like you're doing now.'

She wanted to protest and say that she wasn't shaking, and that the other responses he had mentioned were just a figment of his self-deluded ego. But if she did that then they'd both know that she was guilty of doing what he had accused her of doing a few moments ago. Telling lies.

He was playing with her just for his own warped sense of satisfaction, she guessed, feeling the burn of humiliating tears sting the backs of her eyes again, and she knew she had to get out of there before she showed herself up completely.

'Goodbye, Andreas.'

He was at the door, blocking her exit, even before she had time to reach for the handle.

'Do you really think I asked you up here just for my own amusement?' he drawled, startling her with how close he had come to reading her thoughts. But then—as he had said—he *knew* her, didn't he?

'You didn't *ask*.'

'All right, I brought you up here,' he amended casually, as though it was of no consequence. 'But at the time you didn't seem in a fit state to handle anything else.'

His eyes were raking over her face as though looking for signs of her earlier weakness, but his subtle reference to that kiss they had shared earlier was far too disconcerting and Magenta swallowed, taking a step back.

'Do you have a point?'

That smile touched his lips again as he moved around her, away from the door.

'Ah, the same old Magenta. Always cutting to the chase.'

'I'm in a hurry.'

'Of course. Your other interviews.' His tone mocked. 'However, despite all your accusations and suspicions regarding my ulterior motives, there *is* another position becoming vacant in this company.'

'There is?' Magenta's heart gave a little leap of hope, although she was still viewing him with suspicion.

'Another PA is taking an indefinite spell of leave,' he told her with a grimace. 'Rather sooner than we expected her to. We haven't yet found anyone suitable to fill the post.'

'And you're offering *me* the position?' Something like relief started to trickle through her veins. Could this mean that there was an end in sight to her endless and ever-increasing money worries? That she wouldn't be forced to impose on her great-aunt's generosity when Josie had given so much of herself already?

'Why so surprised, Magenta? Your CV looks promising, if a little lacking in experience, and it does say that you can start right away. The PA in question is taking time off to look after her mother during a period of scheduled surgical operations and she's expected to be away for four or five months. She's the one, incidentally, whom you were trying very hard not to let me catch you looking at in the bar the other night. I was trying to talk her out of going so soon, but circumstances dictate that I have to be a gentleman about it and comply with her wishes. In short, Magenta, you'll be working for *me*.'

A tremulous little laugh left her lips—something between amazement and utter disbelief. 'Tell me you're joking?' A crushing disappointment was replacing her premature relief.

'I never joke about business matters.'

'Why? *Why,* when you so obviously don't like me, would you want to employ me?'

'You know…I've asked myself that very question,' he said.

He moved closer to her—close enough to reach out and lift her chin between his thumb and forefinger. His warmth seared her skin, making her catch her breath.

'And?' It came out as a croak. She was trying not to let him affect her, trying not to breathe in the tantalising freshness of his cologne.

He shrugged. 'I need an assistant. You're looking for a position.'

'I had a position—or as good as,' she interjected. 'Until you came and snatched it from me.'

His hand fell away from her, although his eyes never left her face. 'Well, maybe I'm just nursing a masochistic need to have you working for me.'

'So you can remind me every day of how badly I treated you?' *If* she had treated him badly. *Think!* she urged herself, but nothing would come.

Andreas's laugh was infused with irony. 'I thought I made that clear when I saw you last Friday? Your actions in the past left no indelible marks.'

'Well, that's all right, then, isn't it?' she breathed, silently disturbed by his chilling declaration. 'And you'd still take me on after you've intimated that the job I was applying for was out of my league. This is obviously a far more responsible position, and you've already said I'm lacking in experience. What makes you imagine I'm up to meeting all your requirements?'

'Oh, you'll meet them, Magenta. Rest assured about that.'

He wasn't saying anything, but something in the dark penetration of his eyes made her shiver. Somehow he didn't seem to be just talking about his requirements of a PA.

'Well, thanks, but no thanks,' she said, turning away.

'You'll walk away knowing that the lease on your flat is hanging in the balance and that you don't even have the resources to renew it?'

She swung round to face him, the tears she had been fighting since the moment he'd strode in and ripped all her hopes apart now glistening unashamedly in her eyes. 'How did you know that?'

'You've just confirmed it,' he said. 'Apart from which one of my colleagues who attended your first interview mentioned the letter that you asked for.'

'The letter?' she murmured, and was suddenly mortifyingly aware of what he meant.

She'd made a fool of herself at that first interview by prematurely believing, from the way the conversation was going, that they were already offering her the job. She'd been so desperately relieved that she'd asked if she could have their offer in a formal letter, which she could pass on to her landlord's agents. It didn't take half a brain—let alone a keen mind like his—to work out the reason why.

'So you decided to capitalise on my misfortune?'

'I'm offering you a job.'

'Not the sort I'm willing to take.'

'On the contrary, Magenta. I think you'll take any job you can get. And may I point out that I'm not the one implying anything improper? You are.'

'You're not?'

'No. And I'm not sure what you're getting so falsely modest and indignant about,' he stated. 'It wouldn't be the first time you'd sold yourself to the highest bidder.'

It was obvious that he believed what he was saying, and that he would never cease to remind her of it or to exact retribution for it—which was the only reason, she was sure, that he was offering her the position now.

'I've never *sold* myself!' she emphasised, trying to ignore the goading little voice inside her head that was asking, *How do you know?* 'I haven't,' she reiterated, trying to convince herself in spite of it. 'And I'm not selling myself to you, Andreas,' she tagged on. But there was desolation in her eyes as she realised that for her own sake, and especially for Theo's welfare, she had very little choice but to accept his offer.

His mouth compressed with evident satisfaction as a knock on the door announced the arrival of the coffee.

'Well, we'll see, shall we?' he said, knowing as well as she did that she was beaten.

CHAPTER THREE

MAGENTA WOKE WITH a start, sweating and trembling. She
had been dreaming that she was looking for something and
didn't even know what it was, but as the trembling subsided
and the fog lifted from her brain things started to become a
little clearer.

She had been sobbing while she was asleep because of
something she had lost and desperately wanted back, but it
wasn't anything tangible that she had been looking for. She
knew it had been something to do with Andreas....

She was lying on top of the bed, where she had slumped,
drained and exhausted, after coming home from that inter
view today and after that unsettling time in his office. She'd
remembered so much. The restaurant. His father and grandmother. Even snatches of their brief but tempestuous affair.
But there were aspects of their relationship that still continued to elude her. Like what had happened to make him so
hostile towards her? Had it been to do with her modelling
career? And why was he so convinced that Marcus Rushford
was Theo's father?

Think!

She lay there for a while, until her brain felt fit to burst,
and then with a frustrated groan forced herself off the bed
and into the bathroom.

Her body had changed very little since her teenage years,

she thought, catching a glimpse of the tall, slender figure in
the mirror. And ever since she had grown up her unusual
looks had attracted far more attention from the opposite sex
than she'd wanted or encouraged—and because of it a name
she hadn't even earned.

Stepping into the shower, Magenta thought reluctantly of
how her mother's reputation hadn't helped. With no father,
and no knowledge of any, she recalled that she'd had a string
of 'uncles' who had drifted in and out of her young life. Her
mother had been unable to maintain a steady relationship
with any man. One disastrous affair after another had led to
her seeking solace by drinking too much, and it had been her
daughter who had always borne the brunt of it. Add the stigma
of her birth poverty, because Jeanette James had never been
able to work, and Magenta's schooldays had been hard—both
at home and in the classroom. Somehow she had never quite
fit in with her classmates, and consequently had never made
friends easily. For that reason she had grown up wanting to
rise above the situation she was in. And because of her face
and figure—both accidents of birth—a modelling career had
seemed the only way to do it.

Her physical attributes together with her background,
however, had caused men to expect more from her, Magenta
thought bitterly, than she'd been prepared to give. But she
had resisted them all until...

By instinct alone she knew that there had only ever been
one man who had set her body on fire, and that man was Andreas Visconti. But everything he had said to her today—and
the other night in the wine bar—implied the contrary. For
some reason he truly believed that she had had some sort of
sexual liaison with Marcus Rushford....

As she lathered soap over her body a picture of a room
and then a whole apartment rose before her mind's eyes. A
coldly furnished, expensive apartment. Marcus's! she realised, shocked. She had been staying there. No, not stay-

ing. *Living* there, she thought, shaking her head to induce more of the same troubling recollections. But try as she did her memory refused to oblige. Whatever it was that still remained buried, she knew that it fell within a definite period. And that was the nine or ten months prior to the day just over five years ago when her mother had woken up unusually early and found her collapsed on the bathroom floor.

Her cell phone was ringing just as she was stepping out of the shower, and Magenta raced over and snatched it off the windowsill.

'Hello, darling.' Emotion welled up inside her until she thought her heart would burst just from hearing her little son's voice.

'Aunt Josie asked me to ask you if you got the job.'

Of course. She'd talked of nothing else for weeks, she reflected, shrugging into her robe and thinking of the better life she had told Theo she'd be able to give him if she was lucky enough to get through the interview—of the new football boots and the *Thomas the Tank Engine* duvet cover she had promised him.

She shuddered as she thought of how—almost—she had had no job at all, and wondered how she would have coped if Andreas had blocked her chances of working for his company altogether. If he hadn't gone on to offer her the temporary position she had finally agreed to take.

'Tell Aunt Josie I didn't take that one because I got an even better one.' She tried to sound excited, although she didn't know what could be *better* about securing a job that put her immediately under a man who had no reservations about showing how much he despised her. Except the money...

Selling herself to the highest bidder.

She shivered, wondering if by agreeing to work for him she wouldn't be playing right into Andreas's hands.

She had to take this job—she didn't have any choice. Even if she was still dangerously and unbelievably attracted to him, and even though he was displaying a ruthless desire to get even with her.

But was he going to use her vulnerability and her attraction to him to do it? she wondered, with a contrary mix of apprehension and excitement. Everything about him had suggested he intended to when she had been in his office today. If he was, she thought, she only hoped she would be strong enough emotionally to resist him. At least taking this job might help to restore her memory—even if she had a deep-rooted anxiety inside about what remembering might reveal....

Andreas had arranged to pick Magenta up the following Monday morning, and he noticed the curtains twitch in an upstairs window as he pulled up outside a characterless nineteen-seventies semi-detached house which, from the two doorbells beside the rather jaded-looking front door, had obviously been converted into two flats.

Magenta was locking the inner door to the ground-floor flat before he had even made it to the crookedly hung gate, and just the sight of her produced a swift sharp kick to his groin.

She was wearing her hair down this morning. Its rich, dark lustre reminded him of how it had felt to run his fingers through it, and he noticed how much it emphasised the porcelain-like texture of her skin. With that hair, those thick black lashes and those dark eyes she had a look that was almost as continental as his own ancestry. But it was that kissable pouting mouth that today she'd enhanced with a subtle pink lip cream that was doing untold things to his libido, and he had to force his gaze down. That didn't improve matters, because then all he could think about was the beautiful slim body underneath the black pencil skirt and tailored jacket of which he knew every delicious and delectable inch.

'Keen to make a good impression, Magenta?' His reluctant awareness of her forced him to say it, but he was irritated at the power she still had to affect him physically as he leaned against the long, low-slung silver Mercedes, watching her approach.

'No. I just don't like to keep anyone waiting.'

It was a cool, unflustered response. Remarkably unflustered, he noted, opening the passenger door for her.

'Thanks.'

She didn't meet his eyes as she said it—probably because she'd had to pass so close to him, he decided. Close enough for him to catch the subtle yet sensuous perfume she was wearing.

Not so unflustered, he thought smugly, noticing the quickened rise of her breasts beneath her pale grey camisole, as well as the nervous little movement of her throat. A silver-set ebony pendant lay against its pulsing hollow, attached to the silver torque she wore around her neck today.

He wondered at this fascination she had with scarves and chokers and accessories. She'd always worn things like that with reluctance when she'd been going somewhere special, or her outfit had demanded it, and she'd always ripped them off as soon as he'd taken her home, proclaiming that jewellery of any kind made her feel cluttered. It was with tantalising decorum, he remembered, that whenever they were alone she'd always waited for *him* to remove her clothes.

'I thought I would have the chance of meeting your son this morning,' he expressed after he had put the car in motion. His voice was slightly hoarse from the direction his thoughts had taken. She'd told him only that she had adequate childcare when he had challenged her about it the other day; when he had reminded her that they were only just at the start of the school summer holiday.

She was stealing covert little glances around the interior of his car, as though she couldn't quite believe how successful he had become.

'No. He's away for two weeks.'

'With your mother?' He couldn't think of a less suitable candidate to look after a five-year-old child, and thought it was probably for the best that the boy's father didn't know about it. Had *he* been in the man's shoes, he couldn't help thinking grimly, he would have taken immediate steps to do something about it. 'How is she, by the way?'

She spared him a glance that seemed to challenge why he was asking. There had been no love lost between Jeanette James and his family ever since the day the woman had come into the restaurant, the worse for drink, to accuse his grandmother of spreading gossip about Magenta. She had probably guessed he was only asking because protocol demanded it.

'She's fine—and she's living with her partner in Portugal,' she told him sketchily, deciding not to enlarge upon how much better her mother seemed since meeting a man who had kept her on the right road after coming round to paint her flat three years ago. 'Theo's gone away for a couple of weeks with my great-aunt to her stepdaughter's in Devon. They've got sons a similar age to Theo.'

'I didn't know you had a great-aunt.' He was slowing down to let another car out of a side turning, but he sent a questioning glance at her when he sensed her hesitation in answering.

'Just because I didn't mention her, it doesn't mean she didn't exist,' she said as he brought the car back up to speed again.

'Do I take it she's your mother's aunt?'

'That would be the most natural assumption, since I don't have the first idea who my father was.'

And that was something that had always chafed, he reflected, picking up on the familiar defensive note in her voice.

'So she's more like a grandmother?'

'Yes.'

'And naturally she's getting on in years?'

'Meaning…?'

Her dark eyes were challenging again, and he wished he

had been able to contain his criticism. But it was too late. All he could do was continue along the same track.

'Meaning is it really fair to expect someone of her age to take on the responsibility for your child? Especially one so young? Has she had children of her own? Any experience in looking after infants?'

'She should,' she returned tartly, 'she brought him up for the first—' She cut short whatever it was she had been about to say.

'For the first what, Magenta?' he asked, slicing a steel-hard glance across the air-conditioned space that separated them. 'Just how long did you stand by and allow someone else to bring up your child?'

She was sitting staring out of the windscreen, looking tense and rigid, with her pale pink nails almost digging into the soft leather bag she was clutching on her lap.

Had she really put her career before her baby? A muscle twitched in his clenched jaw as he gave his attention to the road again. If so, what was it that had finally made her stop? He wasn't even sure he wanted to know.

'Where are we going?'

For the first time since she had got into his car, bowled over again by how well he had done for himself and by that air of authority he wore as effortlessly as he wore those dark executive clothes, Magenta realised that he wasn't taking her to his office. Distractedly she'd noticed the sign for the only route they should have taken well over a couple of miles back, and now he'd crossed over into the lane that would take them to the motorway.

'I'm taking you back to the house because there are things in my diary I need to go over with you.'

'The house?' *His* house? Magenta swallowed, wondering exactly where he lived. Before she knew it she was blurting out, 'Over my dead body.'

'You're my PA. You do as I instruct. Or weren't you aware that that was one of the conditions of your employment?'

His sarcasm rankled, but Magenta bit her tongue to stop humiliating herself still further. Whatever they had been, she thought, he was now her boss and she was just his employee. There was no getting away from the fact.

'Aye aye, sir,' she snapped, still riled by how he had automatically assumed that she had let her mother—of all people!—raise Theo while she...what? Pursued a glamorous career? Or did he imagine she'd whiled away her time in some rich man's paradise?

She knew he already had a low opinion of her. What she couldn't take was him—or anyone—thinking that she was an uncaring mother as well.

Her pride kept her from telling him how wrong he was, and why she hadn't been able to look after her own baby—share in his upbringing—for the first few months of his life. If he wanted to think the worst about her, then let him, she decided resignedly. He didn't know anything about her—least of all that Theo was his. That same surfacing fear reinforced her decision not to take a chance on telling him. If he wanted to hurt her, for whatever reason he was harbouring in his mind, then that would give him all the ammunition he needed. And if his derogatory comments today about Theo's care were anything to go by, she had no doubt he would do everything in his power to take her son away from her.

The gates through which the car had swung revealed a mansion of breath-catching style. A modern white house in Georgian design, with clean lines and perfect symmetry, its wide arched doorway was centre-set within an abundance of long, multi-paned windows, and its drive gave on to manicured lawns and grounds that meandered away to the woods. Magenta even glimpsed a tennis court towards one side of the house.

'This is...yours?' She knew she sounded awestruck, but she couldn't help it. She had already realised he'd become rich. The company and the car had told her that much. But she hadn't fully realised until now just how rich he was.

'Not bad for a lad who was never going to amount to anything, mmm?'

Was that what she had said? Knowing herself as she did, she couldn't believe she ever could have, but from the way he had said it, and that self-satisfied look on his face as he came around the bonnet to where she stood, dumbfounded by his beautiful house, she obviously must have.

'And you're obviously enjoying rubbing it in.' If it was true, then it would be no more than she deserved, Magenta accepted, wondering just how long he intended to make her eat humble pie.

'Come on.'

His arm was fleeting across her shoulders, but surprisingly Magenta felt the loss of it with a keenness that made her almost ache as he brought her across the pale shingle of the drive. As she walked with him her senses were awakening to the familiarity of his stride, the way his body moved beside hers, the intonations of his voice, and she felt herself responding to them with an ease that was as stimulating as it was scary.

He opened the impressive front door and let her into his home. It was a house filled with light and space, exclusive furnishings and fine art. In the wide reception hall and in the sumptuously furnished drawing room into which he showed her fine silverware on polished surfaces threw back reflections of the sunny morning through the floor-to-ceiling windows. A display of old-fashioned amber roses graced a crystal vase in the centre of a Regency table, their scent so sweet it seemed to permeate every inch of air space in the luxurious room.

'They're my favourite flowers.'

Images rushed up in her, so vivid she had to grasp the tall back of one of the richly upholstered chairs to try and steady herself. Each deep breath she took was filling her lungs with the heady, evocative perfume... Andreas giving her roses... amber roses from his grandmother's flowerbed...

She glanced up and saw him watching her. His eyes were smouldering with a dark intensity that had her looking quickly away, her gaze skittering over a couple of original-looking oil paintings on the wall to the huge windows and the breathtaking view of the eternal grounds beyond.

'Feel free to look around.' Some deep and private emotion seemed to colour his voice. 'I know you're longing to. '

But not as much as he was enjoying being able to show her!

'Bastard!' She didn't know why the invective escaped her, except that it spilled from a well of pent-up frustration with his attitude, from remembering so much and then hitting a blank wall whenever she tried to push her thoughts too far.

'Why?' If his home had made her speechless, then his eyes were holding her spellbound as he moved with the stealth of a stalking cat across the pastel-tinted Turkish carpet that graced the pale oak floor. 'For refusing to stay in the lowly situation you clearly saw me in? For having the gall to claw my way to the top?'

'I can't image you clawing your way out of anywhere, Andreas. Fighting, maybe—metaphorically speaking. Or slaying anyone who stood in your way.'

He laughed that soft laugh that seemed to ring alarm bells in Magenta. But then he reached out and gently tilted her chin with his finger.

For a moment, with his penetrating eyes probing the wary depths of hers, silence seemed to wrap them in some sort of sensual bubble. She was aware of a clock ticking quietly on the white marble mantelpiece, the poignant scent of the roses, and Andreas's steady breathing that seemed to mock the rapidity of her own.

Her breath seemed to stand still as his fingers trailed lightly down her throat, but then his fingers curled around the open-backed torque and gently tugged at the clinging silver, bringing Magenta's hand slamming down over his.

'Take it off,' he ordered softly.

'No.'

'Six years ago I wouldn't have needed to ask.'

'Six years ago we were different people.' They must have been, otherwise how would she have found the nerve to take him on? she wondered. Let alone try and cross him— humiliate him? And if everything he had intimated was true then that was what she had done.

'Really?' An elevated eyebrow assured her that he didn't believe it. 'Do people really change that much?'

No longer trying to rid her of her necklace, his fingers were now playing along the sensitive skin beneath the heavy curtain of her hair, his touch so light that Magenta's lids came down against the exquisite yet dangerously stirring action. She could feel his eyes on her face—glacial eyes, reflecting a chilling satisfaction because he knew how he was affecting her.

Now, with her eyes flickering open, and in response to what he had just said about people changing, she was startled to hear herself utter a simple yet heartfelt, 'You have.'

'Yes, well…' he breathed, just as his cell phone started to ring.

He turned away, taking his phone out of his pocket and answering his caller with brisk efficiency, as though Magenta were the last thing on his mind.

However she remembered him being before, he was cold and cynical now, and she listened to him speak with growing amazement at the authority he wielded. He would command respect, she realised, from the office cleaner right up to his peers at top executive level. Yet she knew instinctively that he would offer them respect in turn.

And because of what had happened in that lift the other day he obviously had no respect for *her* whatsoever, believing she was easy. Believing she was still the same girl who had…what? Left him for some other man?

She was standing by the window when he finished speaking on the phone, re-energising her spirits with the peace and serenity of the sunny gardens. There were a couple of willows beyond the lawns, their graceful boughs overhanging what had to be a narrow body of water winding its way through his property. Closer to hand, the tennis court looked inviting enough to make her want to play. Across the terrace, which swept down and wrapped itself around the other side of the house, she glimpsed a pool area, half hidden by trees, its clear blue water sparkling beneath the glittering sky.

'Andreas…' she began, tensing at the soft sound of his approach over the luxurious carpet. 'Just because I—I was stupid enough to—to get carried away in that lift the other day, don't—' She was losing the fluency of her speech, just as she had in the early days during and after her spell in hospital, and she gritted her teeth, her fingers clenched like curled claws sinking painfully into her palms. *Dear Heaven! Don't let me fall apart now!*

'Don't what?' he enquired, his face a mask of questioning complexity.

'Don't think I'm easy.'

He uttered one of those low, sexy laughs, his brows drawing together as his gaze slid downwards.

Surprising her, he caught her hand and dragged it up, unfolding her tight, tense fingers. His hooded eyes took in the red half-moons her nails had left in the soft flesh and she caught her breath as he suddenly dipped his head and pressed his lips to the angry marks.

'I promise you I won't do anything you don't want me to do,' he murmured, his breath warm and recklessly exciting against her palm. 'Now, let's get to work.'

He was the CEO again, speaking to her as he would to any employee—as he had to that caller on the phone—confident in the knowledge that he only had to touch her to make her want him to do all sorts of things to her. Because she had shown him he could....

She somehow knew she had never been able to control the way her body responded to him, and simply prayed that she was mature enough now to be able to resist his devastating masculinity—just as he appeared to be able to resist her. Otherwise where would she and Theo be, if circumstances made it impossible for her to stay on and work for him and she found herself having to give up this job?

His study was at the other end of the huge house, and as well equipped as any modern office. A smaller room right next to it was fitted with filing cabinets and a desk where his PA could work. Both rooms enjoyed a fuller aspect of the poolside.

Magenta spent the morning going through his diary with him, rearranging and confirming meetings over the telephone, and generally tidying up files and correspondence.

'What made you so sure you were right in your assumption about my...circumstances?' she challenged, albeit hesitantly, as she was nibbling a biscuit with her coffee. It had been brought in by a middle-aged housekeeper who had smiled warmly at Magenta while maintaining an air of detachment that respected her employer's privacy. 'I could have asked for that letter simply because...well, because I had my eye on some luxurious and exciting new place to live.'

From behind his desk he gave her a look that suggested she wouldn't have been working as she had been if she'd had that much money to throw around. 'I always make it my business to learn as much as I can about anyone I'm intending to have working closely with me.'

'So you intended it? Even before I got to that final interview?'

Jacketless, his tie loosened beneath his opened collar, he was picking up his mug, his fingers long and tanned around the pale glaze. 'As I said, I never leave anything to chance.'

'Did you know on that Friday? When we bumped into each other in the wine bar?'

He made a rather cynical sound down his nostrils. 'I didn't have a clue. Not until I noticed your name on the shortlist on Monday morning.

'So how did you get the low-down on my situation? Through extra-sensory perception?'

He finished his coffee, looking composed and relaxed as he laid his mug aside. 'Even I can't claim to have *that* particular gift at my disposal.'

'How, then?' she demanded as she swallowed the last of her biscuit. Inside she was feeling exposed and vulnerable, and she was wishing that he wasn't doing funny things to her just by sitting there looking so disgustingly handsome.

'It isn't important.' He sat back on his chair. 'Only that you're here.'

'It is. That information was confidential.' She dumped her mug down on his desk. 'Whoever told you, they had absolutely no right!'

'Maybe not,' he drawled laconically. 'But I've found that in this world anyone will tell you anything if you make it worth their while. Your landlord's agents being no exception.'

'Bribe them, you mean?'

He chuckled low in his throat. 'You *do* have a low opinion of me,' he drawled.

Magenta surveyed him with narrowed eyes, her head tilting slightly. 'No lower than your opinion of me. So what did you do? Ring them and ask what the situation was on the flat that's got the "To Let" sign outside?'

He didn't answer as he stretched out his arms, flexing his fingers before cupping them behind his head.

'You're unscrupulous,' she breathed.

'And you aren't?'

For wanting a career? She didn't say it, although she knew instinctively that it was something to do with that, and it was a long moment after his rather scathing remark before she spoke again.

'Whatever I did that you think was so bad, I was nineteen,' she reminded him, thinking about asking him to spell it out for her, but deciding to bluff her way around it instead. 'And, despite what you said, people *do* change.'

'In that case I'm looking forward to a very enlightening few months,' he said.

There was definitely something different about Magenta, Andreas thought, watching from the window and waiting with growing impatience for his caller to ring off so that he could go out into the garden and join her.

She'd gone outside after finishing the tea and sandwiches his housekeeper had sent in, telling him she needed some fresh air. Now, as he watched her looking up at a kestrel that was gliding over the garden, he realised that she had the power to fascinate him as she was fascinated by that bird. She was drawing him in with her dangerous attraction even more strongly than she had in the past. But something had changed...

For a girl who was once very conscious of the way she looked, always retouching her make-up and absently playing with her thick, lustrous hair, she seemed remarkably oblivious to her femininity. She seemed more reserved too than the effervescent nineteen-year-old who had gone a long way to destroying his faith in her sex. Then there was that hesitancy he noticed when she was speaking sometimes, as though she wasn't too sure of herself—although he was certain that it wasn't through a lack of confidence.

Listening to her speaking to his colleagues and clients

over the phone this morning, he had been impressed with her charm and her efficiency. But there was something about her. Something he couldn't quite put his finger on…

His call took too long and she was already in the hall by the time he was able to join her.

'My grandmother,' he informed her, noticing her interest in the small oval framed oil painting hanging above one of the Georgian tables. 'As a young woman.'

'She was very beautiful.'

'Yes.'

'Is she still—?' She broke off, as though deciding it was too imprudent to ask.

'No,' he informed her. 'She died last year in Italy, without a day's illness, after a very long and active eighty-nine years.'

The eyes that met his were dark and guarded. 'I'm sorry— and about your father too.'

'Yes.' He exhaled deeply as he said it. 'So am I.'

'What happened?' she asked, sounding as tentative as her eyes were wary.

'A heart attack.'

'When?'

'Six years ago.'

'Six years…' He saw her velvety brows come together. 'When you were in America?'

'Before I left,' he told her succinctly.

What he didn't add was that it had been only hours after she'd been round to see him and they had parted for the final time. Or that they had been arguing because of *her*. The remorse and regret he carried because of it were constant companions deep within him, along with the scouring knowledge that if he had listened to his father the man would probably still be alive today.

Her frown was deepening and she started to say something else, but he cut across her. 'Let's have done with the reminiscing, shall we?' he said abruptly.

* * *

'I'm going to be working at home for the next week or so,' Andreas told her as he brought the Mercedes to a standstill outside her flat that evening. 'And as you don't have your own transport—' he had already learned that she didn't own a car '—I think it would be far more convenient if you stayed there too.'

About to get out of the car, Magenta viewed him with disbelief. 'You didn't say anything about staying under your roof when I agreed to take this job.'

Clicking on the handbrake, he turned off the engine before swivelling round on his seat to face her. 'Well, I'm saying it now. I've got several meetings, all based within a twenty-mile radius on the wrong side of the office, and I'm afraid I'm going to need you with me for at least two of them. Those are the terms.'

'Does your usual PA—or any of your other staff,' she tagged on, thinking of the obviously smitten Lana Barley-thorne, 'always bow to your command and move in with you whenever you snap your fingers?'

'I'm hardly snapping my fingers, so don't go convincing yourself you have no choice in the matter,' he advised, effectively taking her down a peg. 'And I think you need reminding that you aren't my regular PA—or any other loyal and long-standing member of my workforce.' His tone implied that she was never likely to be. 'So stop making a fuss, pack a bag, and I'll pick you up at eight tomorrow morning. After all, you told me your son's away, so it isn't as though there's anyone you have to get back for. Or is there?' he enquired, with curiosity suddenly underlying the cynicism in his voice.

'I don't really think that's any of your concern,' Magenta retaliated, and immediately wished she hadn't. If he hadn't offered her this extremely well-paid position then she and Theo would have been out on the street at the end of next month.

'Will there be anything else?' She almost added, *sir,* but decided that might be pushing things a little too far.

'Yes. It's promising to be a sizzling week ahead, so bring a swimsuit,' he instructed, causing Magenta's stomach to flip as she stepped out of the car.

Somehow, she thought, letting herself in through the rickety metal gate, she didn't think he was just talking about the weather.

CHAPTER FOUR

A CHAUFFEUR-DRIVEN car arrived for Magenta at eight o'clock sharp the following morning. A long, dark saloon with tinted windows. She knew it would start the neighbours speculating, even without the dark uniformed man who rang her bell.

'Mr Visconti has an early appointment and won't be around until later, but I'm to take you to the house and see that you're settled in before he gets in.'

'Thank you,' Magenta said, stepping through the back passenger door with a little pang of misgiving. This was certainly some way to travel. But she was beginning to feel more like some rich man's mistress than a temporary personal assistant, and with a little tingle of something she didn't want to question too fully she considered that that was probably exactly what Andreas was intending her to feel.

The privacy panel was up and, grateful for it, Magenta wasted no time in ringing her great-aunt's cell phone. It was Theo who answered, just as she'd hoped he would.

'Hello, darling.' She was missing him dreadfully and told him so, without revealing just how much. His childhood was to be enjoyed, not dogged by adult worries and problems as her own had been. 'You'll never believe the car Mummy's sitting in,' she enthused brightly and, knowing his passion for anything with wheels, went on to tell him all about it.

'Be careful, my girl,' Aunt Josie warned when she took

over the conversation and Magenta told her that she was going to be working at her new boss's home for the next few days. 'I know you said you knew him years ago, but—well…he's still a man…and a very good-looking and eligible one from what you've told me about him.'

'You don't have to worry about me, Aunt Josie,' Magenta assured her, in a way in which she couldn't reassure herself. She could visualise her mother's aunt, her iron-grey hair slightly ruffled, wearing her 'Home is where the Hearth is' apron, which Magenta had bought last Christmas and which she was never without, even when she went to visit her stepdaughter. 'You've done enough of that over the past five years. Besides, I'm perfectly able to take care of myself nowadays.'

'I still worry,' her great-aunt replied. 'Especially when my favourite girl is involved with a man who's rich and no doubt charming enough to get anything he wants.'

Warmed by her motherly concern, Magenta laughed—although a crease was deepening between her eyes. She'd told Aunt Josie about knowing Andreas before when she'd informed her that she had got the job. She had been too fazed, however, by those almost debilitating snatches of memory and the equally weakening battle to try and make sense of images and fragments of conversation that still continued to elude her to tell her anything else. Nor was she prepared yet, with one of his staff within earshot—even if he might not be able to hear her through the transparent screen and above his softly playing radio—to let anyone who didn't have to know in on the fact that she and Andreas had been lovers. She didn't want to risk anyone sharing in her humiliation when he cast her off, as she knew he would sooner or later, whether he'd settled the score he felt he had to settle or not.

The suite of rooms she was shown into when she arrived at Andreas's mansion was, like the rest of the place, luxuriously furnished, with deep-piled Turkish rugs, designer fabrics gracing the expansive bed and long, multi-paned windows. The bathroom, with its pale, exquisitely tiled floor and matching walls, displayed a huge, free-standing bathtub and a gleaming white suite in Italian marble that promised to pamper her with the highest level of indulgence.

The bedroom had three deep windowsills where she could sit and look out onto the grounds and acres of sprawling countryside beyond. The air coming in through the window where Magenta had paused to take in the view was heavy with the scent of a climbing red rose, overlaid with the occasional hint of wild honeysuckle.

She could have sat there all day, but she knew she couldn't linger long and went down to the study. Andreas wasn't back yet, so she went through to the smaller office and immersed herself in her work, tidying up files and handling any correspondence she could deal with in his absence.

She was just winding up a conversation with a local councillor who was clarifying a question about building regulations within the site of a new hotel when Andreas walked in.

'How long have you been here? Since three this morning?'

He looked genuinely impressed as he came over and flipped through the tray of letters and copy e-mails she had printed off for posting or filing, his gaze taking in the pile of orderly files that were ready to be put away. It gave her a ridiculously warm glow inside.

'Just doing my job,' she murmured, swivelling round on her chair and whipping another page of perfectly typed, perfectly worded text out of the printing tray, trying not to let her pleasure show.

'In that case I think you've done enough for one morning. It's twenty-seven degrees out there and it's nearly lunchtime. Time, I think, to fit in a pre-lunch swim.'

'If it's all the same to you, I'd rather finish this e-mail,' Magenta answered, trying to ignore her body's response to Andreas in his short-sleeved white shirt, tie and light grey hip-hugging trousers, even though she knew she was fighting a losing battle. His scent alone—a heady blend of pine coupled with warm, masculine skin—was working on her senses and making her far too aware of herself. And of him.

'The e-mail can wait,' he advised, in a tone that was quietly impatient. 'Go and change. Or didn't you do as I suggested yesterday and bring a swimsuit?'

'I did what I felt comfortable doing,' Magenta told him pointedly, letting him know from the outset that she wasn't going to be bullied or browbeaten into doing anything she wasn't happy with. That over with, she tagged on, 'Yes, I brought a swimsuit.'

'Then will you be my guest, Miss James...' his dark head tilting, he all but bowed '...and kindly consent to join me in the pool?'

'Don't overdo it.' His excessive attempt at courtesy lent her mouth a wry twist as she pushed herself to her feet and started towards the door.

'And Magenta?'

She glanced back over her shoulder, her hair a rich ebony curtain against her face.

'Get rid of the scarf.'

It was only a whisper of cream gossamer silk, which she had worn to complement her bronze collarless blouse and cream suit, but it was obviously irritating him immensely.

'Get rid of it,' he said softly. 'Otherwise I really will be obliged to remove it myself.'

The suggestion of his touching her, in any way whatsoever, sent a throb of tension pulsing along her veins. It had been second nature once to have him undress her. She remembered that much—and vividly. Now, though, the excitement generated by the thought of letting him was overlaid with an almost sickening fear. Fear of her vulnerability. Of knowing that if she did she would be playing right into his hands. Fear of his seeing the marks on her body that would give rise to a lot of questions, and fear that in a weak moment she might even tell him the truth about Theo.

And if she did that...

She had survived a lot, but she didn't think she would survive if he took her son away from her, and the only way to ensure that he didn't was to remain immune. He didn't like her, and therefore it was imperative that she resisted whatever plan of seduction he might be carefully mapping out for her, she thought, as she pulled on her swimsuit in front of the pearly wardrobes that filled a whole wall of the luxurious dressing area annexed to her bedroom. But as she caught a glimpse of herself in one of the floor-to-ceiling mirrors she could see the way her body was betraying her in the flush across her pale cheeks and in the pink burgeoning peaks of her small breasts.

Andreas was already in the pool when Magenta came down. Chest-deep in water, his face upturned to the sun, he was leaning with his bronzed arms outstretched on the warm marble tiles behind him. His eyes were closed and yet he sensed her presence as tangibly as the sun that was caressing his face and the warm breeze that brought with it the evocative scent of his favourite honeysuckle. Lazily, his eyelids drifted apart.

He had seen her naked before, so it wasn't as if there were any surprises in seeing her scantily dressed. But the years hadn't tempered his hot-blooded desire for her. He had realised that in the wine bar, and again in the lift, when he'd been unable to contain how she made him feel. But never had he wanted her more than he wanted her at this minute, when she was wearing the most demure and yet the sexiest swimsuit his fevered brain could ever have imagined.

Virginal white, it encased her throat in a collar of see-through mesh that extended down across the upper swell of her breasts and continued in a tantalising 'V' which finished just below their silken valley. The stretch fabric of the garment emphasised her still-small waist and slender hips, and the legs were high and cut away, revealing her beautiful lean thighs and shapely calves. Add to that the stark contrast of her hair, which she'd swept up in a loose twist of ebony, and the rather moody, come-hither pout of her lovely mouth, and he was glad that most of his body was under water, so that she wouldn't realise the effect her appearance was having on him.

'Well? Are you going to join me or not?' His voice sounded husky, even to his own ears, but she seemed as tense as he was and didn't seem to notice. Or she was pretending not to, he decided with a wry smile.

The ripple of the water as she slid down off the poolside caressed him in a way that was wholly sensual.

'I see you haven't lost your touch,' he remarked, watching the easy glide of her breaststroke and thinking how gracefully she moved through the water.

'Did you expect me to?' She didn't even turn her head to look at him as she glided effortlessly past.

'With you I learnt a long time ago never to expect anything,' he assured her.

'Anything?'

'Except disappointment and—'

'And what, Andreas?' She kept on swimming. 'Heartache?'

'Heartache?' His laugh seemed almost to taint the peace and beauty of the perfect day as he started swimming after her. 'Nothing so sentimental. I was going to say desire.'

'Desire?' She'd swum over to the side of the pool and now grabbed the tiled edge, using it to propel herself round to face him.

'Sex, if you want it in its most basic definition.'

'I don't.'

'Why not?' A faster, stronger swimmer than she was, he was level with her now. 'Are you going to try and deny that you weren't as hot for me as I was for you? Even more so, if that were possible, judging by your insatiable appetite when you were in my arms.'

The slap that she had itched to administer to that hard cheek the other day now found its target with stinging precision. She heard it and regretted it the instant she saw the water from her errant hand running down his face.

'So you prefer to play rough these days, do you?' he rasped, and the darkening of his eyes promised retribution, sending her front-crawling away from him like a hunted fish.

Andreas's laughter held no warmth as he sliced after her through the clear blue water, catching her easily and curbing her futile attempt to climb out.

'No!'

It was an anguished little sound, strung with panic and something else—something that called to his most primal instincts and sent his testosterone rocketing sky-high. Her eyes were wary yet bright with the same excitement that was driving him as he pulled her round to face him, but the depth of tortured emotion he saw in her face was his total undoing.

'Why did you pretend not to remember me when you saw me in that wine bar, Magenta? What was it you were hoping to gain?'

'Nothing. *Nothing,*' she emphasised, bluffing. 'I was just hoping you would go away.'

'Go away?' He made a derisory sound through his nostrils. 'Did it repel you to speak to me that much?'

Water ran into her eyes and distractedly she brushed it away. Then, standing on tiptoe, she reached up and gently pressed her lips to the spot where her hand had struck him. And that was a mistake, she realised, when he dipped his head and claimed her mouth with his, leaving her rejoicing in her folly as his arms tightened mercilessly around her.

She should stop this madness!

Magenta heard the warning bells clanging away inside her

but took no heed of them as Andreas's mouth became harder and more insistent.

She wanted this! She screamed it silently, in spite of herself, as her body moulded itself of its own accord to the hard planes and angles of his. That physical part of her *knew* him and was recognising its mate, acknowledging him as the other half of a whole that had formed the most fundamental bond, the half that had planted its fertile seed in her willing womb. And she could tell how much he wanted *her*.

His lips and hands were rediscovering her body and she welcomed them like a long lost-part of herself. She had been born to do this with this man, and to know his hands as completely as she knew her own. To carry on his DNA in the shape of her little boy and to be forever lost—her senses only half alive—without the stimulating possession of his kisses.

'How do you get this thing off?'

He was breathing raggedly as he tugged at the restraining fastener at the nape of her neck. One slip of the clasp and he would have her naked in his arms. His to do whatever he wanted with. And she wouldn't have the willpower to resist him. Only the thought of Theo and the resurfacing fear of losing him had her pulling out of those tormenting arms.

'*You* don't!'

With an immense effort of will she struck out for the side of the pool, only the thought of her son keeping her going, and she could already feel the sun-warmed tiles beneath her bare feet by the time Andreas had caught up with her.

'What is it with you, Magenta? Exactly what sort of game do you think you're playing?' The sun was reflecting off his wet, near-naked body like burnished gold.

'No…game.' It was a struggle suddenly even to say that much, and she put a shaky hand to her throbbing head.

'Do you get some warped kick out of turning men on and then switching off the instant you think you've got them hooked, like you did with me first time round? Is that what you did to Rushford? Is it? Is that why he couldn't take any more?'

She knew nothing was further from the truth. How could it be? she agonised. Suddenly she was flinging at Andreas, 'Oh, forget him, will you?'

One side of his mouth lifted in a less than friendly gesture. 'I wish I could. But I'm sorry, darling. Bad memories do tend to die hard.'

Then you should be like me! Magenta screamed silently. *With only half of them intact. See how much you'd like it!*

'And you haven't answered my question. Did you treat him the same way, even though you were pregnant with his child?'

The glare of the sun on the water seemed to be acting like a laser on her tortured head. She heard a deep groan and only realised it came from her own lips a moment before the vibrant pink and greens of the foliage around the poolside splintered into a thousand pieces and she saw indigo tiles rushing up to meet her.

When she opened her eyes she was lying on a bed.

Andreas's bed! she realised at once, from the collection of very masculine furnishings within her sight.

She sat up quickly. Too quickly, she decided, flopping down again when her head swam sickeningly in protest.

'Take it easy.' Andreas's voice above her right shoulder was deep and steadying. It was the only steady thing in the wavering room. 'You passed out and I thought it best to get you inside. How do you feel?'

'Lousy,' Magenta admitted with a grimace, too weak and unbalanced at that moment to try and prevaricate. She was still in her sodden swimsuit, but he had wrapped a towelling robe around her. *His* robe, she realised as things began to settle down. There was the recognisable scent of his cologne clinging to it, along with more elusive traces of his own personal scent. 'It must have been the sun.'

'Possibly, but not very likely.' His sensual mouth pulled

down at one corner. 'Staying up too late, maybe? Or perhaps you just haven't been taking care of yourself properly.'

'What—what do you mean?'

Damn! She wasn't going through a set-back after all these years, was she? she thought in despair, sitting up again, but much more carefully this time. It had taken her months of hard work and effort to perfect her speech in the long battle to reconstruct her life again.

'What are you saying?' She studied him fully now, and wished she hadn't when the sight of him sitting there on the bed in a grey striped silk robe that did little to hide his flagrant masculinity caused a different sort of throbbing in her. 'When her son's away, Magenta will play?' she misquoted. What did he imagine she was doing every night? Having a whale of a time, painting the town bright pink?

'What I meant was that from the way you felt when I carried you up here—like a wisp of nothing—I'd say that you haven't been eating properly.'

'Oh...' she uttered, feeling suitably chastised.

But she didn't tell Andreas that he was right. That lately she had had to be so frugal with her own diet in order to make sure her son had enough to eat that sometimes she'd wound up skipping meals altogether. She hadn't been sleeping properly either, ever since she'd met up with Andreas again, and when she did eventually manage to drop off she was plagued by troubling images that had her waking up trembling and perspiring, struggling to make sense of her disturbing dreams.

'You're just so hunky that any woman would seem light to you,' she parried, trying not to think of how devastating he had looked with his bronze and muscular body all wet and glistening when he'd chased after her out of the pool. 'Besides, I've been a model. I've never quite managed to adopt the desire to over-eat.'

'That's all going to change while you're working for me,' he remonstrated, his hand suddenly palming the curve of a rather too-slender shoulder, where the robe had slipped down, too voluminous for her slim frame.

'You're going to fatten me up?' Her voice sounded squeaky now, but for a different reason. She ached to lean in to his massaging hand. 'Is that another condition of my employment? To put *on* "all those unwanted pounds"?' She dropped her voice as she said it, as if she was advertising some new-fangled slimming product, trying to ignore his casual but very disturbing touch.

'Very necessary pounds,' he corrected. 'I'm not having you passing out on me again at the drop of a hat.'

'That's probably unlikely too, as neither of us wears one,' she quipped, trying to make light of the situation.

She needed to say something to distract her from those lusciously dark-lashed eyes that were using the subject of her weight to examine her with disconcerting thoroughness. His thick black hair was still damp from his swim and she had to stem the almost irresistible urge to run her fingers through it.

'I'm making your bed all wet.' Her voice was husky, and she sounded breathless. But the robe she was wearing was soaking up the water from her swimsuit and it couldn't be doing much for his duvet.

'It wouldn't be the first time,' he said wryly.

Colour touched her cheeks at the significance of what he meant.

'Could I have a shower?'

Thick black brows drew together. 'Are you sure you're up to it?'

She wasn't sure she was, but she needed to get away from him—and fast! 'I think so.'

'Go on, then,' he conceded, getting to his feet so that she could get up off the bed. But as she started towards the door he put a restraining hand on her shoulder. 'No,' he said firmly. 'You'll go in there.' He gestured towards the *en suite* bathroom on the other side of his room. 'That way I can keep an eye on you, just in case you feel inclined to faint on me again.'

Sitting on the bed while she showered and listening to the water cascading down over her lovely body was torture to Andreas, but he was too concerned about her to take himself off to shower in one of the guest bathrooms after what had happened.

But *why* had it happened? The question started up a train of thought that ran away with him as he considered her situation. His colleague had said she'd sounded quite desperate when she'd mistakenly thought she'd been given the job and had asked for that letter for her landlord. Why had things become so difficult for her?

If she'd been modelling since she'd had her son—as she'd implied when she'd accidentally let slip about the child being brought up by her mother's aunt—she would have been earning good money, so where had it all gone? Why was she in such dire straits now?

Her mother had been—and for all he knew still was—totally alcohol-dependent. Could Magenta have gone down the same road? Been swept up in a spiral of parties and social drinking as it was easy to do in the so-called glamorous circles she moved in? Was that why she had claimed not to drink when he had taken her up to his office? Not because of what she'd seen it do to her mother, but because she was in danger of getting hooked on the stuff herself?

Not liking the turn his thoughts were taking, Andreas got up and started pacing the room.

She had driven him nearly insane with her tender femininity in the past. But she had thrown his crazy feelings for her right back in his face. And since then—who knew? What sort of company or practices had she got herself involved with since? She was a woman men couldn't resist. Men and even women—the much older, motherly type—had sometimes stopped him in the street when he had been with her just to congratulate him or comment upon how lovely she was. He'd never experienced anything like it before or since. It had made him feel like a million dollars, knowing how much other men envied him, knowing how much they wanted her when she was his—all his. Except she hadn't been, he reflected, his jaw clenching almost painfully. She wasn't and never had been *his*.

With a sick possessiveness ripping through him he wondered how many men had held her—caressed her—lost themselves in that glorious femininity just as he had—since she had walked out of his life. How many had been made to feel like the only man left in the universe as she'd wrapped those long silky legs around him and fed his ego with her soft impassioned cries? He wondered if he wasn't inviting a whole heap of trouble down on himself by giving her this job, just because he hadn't been able to resist having her under his roof, when he was in danger of being drawn in by her dangerous femininity as hopelessly as he had been six years ago.

He had worked himself into a foul mood and, picking up the phone by the bed, he started dialling a number to try and immerse himself in his work, try and calm himself down.

She was a vamp, a witch, he thought, feeling his body hardening instantly. The sound of water running in the shower had ceased and he glanced towards the bathroom door, aware that she'd be stepping out now, that she'd be towelling herself dry. So what was stopping him from going in there? Dragging the admission from her—even without touching her—that she wanted him as much as he wanted her? He had always been able to arouse her with words in the past so why didn't he just do it? Give in to the promise of sublime ecstasy and instigate what they both wanted? To wind up in that bed together. The duvet was still damply creased with the imprint of her body, and Andreas had to take several deep breaths to engage all his powers of control.

He wouldn't do it because he was much too honourable to
behave like that with a woman. Even a tease who lured men
into her web of unbelievable ecstasy and then dumped them
when it was time to move on to something more profitable.

He was deep in conversation with the manager of one of
his American hotels when Magenta emerged from the bathroom. She'd slipped her arms inside the robe, belted it around
her tiny waist, and with the collar pulled up to meet the damp
loosened tendrils around her face she looked enveloped by it,
so small and waif-like, and yet lovely and desirable.

He made a silent gesture for her to stay when she would
have moved past him and then tried not to focus on her, because the thought of her warm nakedness beneath his robe
was distracting him and his aching libido beyond belief.

Browsing along his bookshelves, while trying to ignore what
the deep timbre of his voice was doing to her, Magenta was
impressed by the diversity of his reading material.

There were beautiful gold-leafed, leatherbound volumes
of an encyclopaedia, travel books—particularly ones about
Italy—several biographies—mainly of business and political
figures—and a whole host of general literature about looking
after the planet, the world's wildlife, as well as the world's
most prized hotels.

Had he read a lot six years ago? She wasn't sure.

'I didn't know you were partial to poetry,' she murmured
when she heard the phone slip back onto its rest. Her head tilting, she noted Lord Byron's name on a comparatively small
and dilapidated-looking little book. 'He's my favourite of all
the romantic poets.'

'Really?' Andreas's voice sounded strange, and he was
looking at her rather oddly. 'You could have fooled me.'

She couldn't fail to pick up on the sarcasm behind his remark. 'You think because I didn't have as good an upbringing as you that I can't appreciate good poetry when I read it?'

she uttered, wondering why he'd even say such a thing. 'We had to study him at school, which is where I developed my taste for romanticism, but this edition's beautiful and so...' *Old,* she was going to say. So old, in fact, that the spine was broken. She reached up to take it down. 'Why don't you have it rebound?'

'Leave it!'

His stern command split the air like the crack of gunshot, freezing her fingers against the dark green suede cover.

'I was only going to look at it,' she told him, defending her actions. 'I wasn't going to...damage it.' Not any more than it was already damaged, she thought, with a pained little crease between her eyes. The throbbing in her head that had been so debilitating earlier was threatening to return again. 'I was just curious to see if I could find my favourite poem.'

'And what is that?'

His tone was clipped and his eyes were coldly questioning— as hard and questioning as the lines that were now corrugating his high forehead.

'I don't know what it's called. It's the poem he wrote to the one woman people say he truly loved.' Funny that she could remember that, Magenta mused, when she had forgotten other, far more important things about her own life. 'I can't...' She put a hand to her head. 'I can't bring the first line of it to mind right now.'

'Try.'

Magenta looked at him quickly, wondering why his voice was so lethally low, and why the glimmer of concern he had shown her before her shower had vanished, to be replaced by what she could only describe as a hard and chilling detachment.

'I don't know...' It was a test she had to pass—for herself as well as Andreas. 'Something about destiny...'

Words and images seemed to be swimming around in a

fog so thick that she couldn't latch onto anything that made sense in her mind.

And then through it Andreas's voice came, like a guiding light through the haze. *"'Though the day of my destiny's over, And the star of my fate hath declined.'"*

That was it! Like someone hypnotised Magenta continued, without taking her eyes off his. *"'Thy soft heart refused to discover, The faults which so many could find...'"*

Her words tailed off, emotion clogging her throat. Had Andreas's heart ever been soft? Yet his eyes were darkening with such an intensity of emotion that it seemed to reach out and touch her. Because, of course, he *had* refused to see the faults in her personality, she remembered startlingly. Even when other people, his family in particular, had condemned her, he had still believed in her, trusted her. Though she knew without any uncertainty, and without even knowing why, that he had condemned her too—in the end.

The emotion was so acute in her chest that she thought she would cry out from the pain of it.

'I need to get dressed.' She struggled to speak in a small, strangled voice, and stumbled away from him before he could make some comment that she couldn't have borne.

He was on the phone, and seemed to wind up the call rather abruptly when he heard her coming into the study, Magenta thought later. He instantly started scribbling something down on a paper pad.

'Why don't you use your iPad?' she suggested rather lamely, feeling awkward and saying the first thing that came into her head because of that tense little episode upstairs earlier.

He didn't even glance up as she spoke, but carried on scribbling with his fine gold pen. 'That's why I'm paying you.'

Of course. He was her boss now, and he was pulling no punches in reminding her of that fact.

'I instructed Mrs Cox to prepare you a light but nutritious lunch,' he went on, with a more than studied glance in her direction now, as she gathered up various forms and other relevant papers she needed from his desk. 'Did she do that?'

Still tense, and smarting from his unnecessary comment a moment ago, she said stiffly, 'Would you rap her over the knuckles and send her packing if I said she didn't?'

In fact she had been given a poached salmon salad with some freshly baked wholemeal bread, a substantial slice of home-made apple pie and cream, and fresh fruit to follow— all which she had devoured with relish. Except the fresh fruit, which she had kept for later.

'Unlike you, my housekeeper doesn't seem to feel the need to oppose me at every given opportunity,' he remarked, his mouth tugging at one corner. 'I would have taken you out to lunch, or at the very least joined you, but in the circumstances I didn't think it would be a good idea.'

He meant because of that moment of weakness which had come over him—over them both—up there in his bedroom earlier. But now he had steeled himself against it—against her—and he couldn't have appeared more controlled and unaffected by her if he had tried.

'No it wouldn't have been,' she said woodenly, pretending to agree with him although she was hurting inside, tormented by the mental pictures that had been plaguing her ever since her shower. *After all, you wouldn't want to risk your reputation by getting too chummy with someone like me!*

He started to say something else, but then the phone on his desk began to ring and he snatched it up.

'Visconti,' he answered, with unusual impatience.

It sounded serious, she thought, closing a file and listening to the tone of his voice, his few clipped responses.

'I've got to go out,' he stated as soon as he had replaced the receiver. Getting up, he grabbed his jacket from the back of his chair. 'I don't know what time I'll be back, so have

any calls you can't deal with personally redirected to my
voice mail.'

And with that he was gone.

Left alone, Magenta waited for the sound of the Mercedes
engine to die away. Then, with the stealth of a fugitive, glancing back every now and then over her shoulder, she crept
swiftly and silently back upstairs to the master suite.

Going across to the bookshelf, she took down the little
suede-covered volume of Byron's poems. Her hand was shaking so much she could hardly turn back the cover. But even
before the inscription in that long, flowing hand leaped out
at her she knew what it was going to say.

For my Magi—with all my love, Andreas

Her hand flew to her mouth to stifle a shuddering gasp.
How could she have forgotten that he had given it to her? He
had addressed it to Magi too, and she suddenly remembered
him saying it, pronouncing the *g* like the softest *j,* with all
the sensuality of his ancestors' native tongue. *My Magi...*

She didn't know why, but she found she was crying silently. And then all at once she knew the reason for it, and
for that sense of loss in those dreams that had been troubling
her over the past few nights. It was because of a lost love.
Andreas's love.

CHAPTER FIVE

ANDREAS'S FACE WAS grim as he stepped out of his marketing manager's office—as grim as it had been when he'd ended that call from her assistant back at the house.

'She's had a late reference in for that girl you took on,' Lana Barleythorne had told him when she had telephoned. 'Magenta James, wasn't it? It seems she's been deliberately holding out on us, and Frances says that there's something about her you should know. She hasn't said what it is—has only intimated that it could be something that might make you want to reconsider your decision to have her working for you.'

He hadn't failed to detect that little note of triumph with which the young woman had said it. He knew Lana had an almost embarrassing crush on him, and he hadn't forgotten how miffed she had seemed when he'd pulled rank on her and the others at Magenta's interview the other day and taken matters right out of their hands.

'She probably hasn't rung you herself yet because she's been tied up in a meeting, but I know she wanted to see you as soon as you came in.'

He had driven like a demon up to the office afterwards, wondering what was so serious that his marketing manager couldn't even share it with her assistant. He'd been wondering about a lot of things. Like the way Magenta had changed. And the way she'd been behaving since their reunion. Like

those bouts of selective amnesia she seemed to fake when
their conversation turned a little bit uncomfortable. Like the
way she'd casually pointed out that poetry book to him today.
She'd acted as though she'd never seen it, let alone had any
knowledge of the ugly scene it had caused between them.
She'd even commented upon its condition, as though she
didn't remember exactly how it had got into that state. As
though she hadn't a clue!

He had planned to quiz her about it over lunch, but when
he'd felt her weaving her dangerous spell around him after
she'd come out of the shower he'd needed an hour or so's
breathing space, had thrown himself into a working lunch
instead. He'd planned to get the truth from her in his office
that afternoon, but just as he'd been about to Lana's call had
come through....

Now, as he drove back through the building rush-hour on
the busy motorway, with the car's air-conditioning system
on full to counteract the heat of the day, he sat grim-faced,
going over all the things he'd wondered about and the things
he now knew.

He'd begun to suspect that if Magenta's memory lapses
weren't faked then she must have embarked on the same
route to destructive self-indulgence as her mother after she'd
walked out of his life. That the problem had to be alcohol-
related...or something worse....

His foot hit the brake pedal, averting a near collision with
the car in front, which had suddenly changed lanes without
warning, nearly taking off his front bumper. With a hard de-
cisiveness he threw on his indicator switch and pulled out
round the offending vehicle, giving himself a clear run ahead.

He'd been certain he was right. In fact by the time he'd
reached his London office he had been convinced of it, he
remembered scathingly, as the big car gobbled up the miles,
bringing him ever closer to her. But what his colleague had
told him in the privacy of that office had made him sick to

his gut, chilling him to the bone. Never in a thousand years could he have suspected what he now knew.

Magenta had stumbled upon the little wooden seat purely by accident. It was situated between the willows and a little stone footbridge spanning a brook, tucked out of sight of the house behind a trellis of wild honeysuckle.

A lovers' seat, she decided. And could no more resist sitting down than she could resist pulling her gypsy-style white blouse off her shoulders and tilting her face to the sun as she soaked up the scent of the flowers and the sound of the brook, the tangible warmth of the late-summer afternoon.

The tranquillity was like balm to the thoughts that had been troubling her ever since Andreas had left and she had crept upstairs to take a proper look at that book.

How could she have forgotten that he had given it to her? she wondered as she waved a rather inquisitive bee away from her hair. It was a special edition that he had bought for her, knowing how much she liked Byron's poetry, and he must have struggled to find the money for it on his meagre salary. But why had he not reminded her of it? Not said *something*? Because surely he must have thought it odd? And what was it doing on his bookshelf, and in such a broken state, when he had clearly meant *her* to have it?

Willing herself to fill in the gaps, she finally gave up and with a sigh of defeat decided to return to the house.

Her heart gave a wild leap as she came out from behind the trellis and almost collided with Andreas.

Tieless, as it had been when he had left the house earlier, his white short-sleeved shirt was half unbuttoned now. His light grey suit jacket was slung casually over one shoulder, and Magenta couldn't help but notice how the superb cut of his trousers emphasised his tight, lean waist and the flat stomach that was testimony to his punishing daily workouts in the pool.

'Magenta.'

She could detect an odd quality to his voice above the gurgling of the brook, even in the way he spoke her name.

'I saw Mrs Cox coming out of the house and she told me I'd probably find you here.'

There was a stark look about his face that released a little dart of unease in her. However, with a broad sweep of her arms, she uttered, 'Well, here I am!'

The movement brought that ice-blue gaze down over her bare, softly tanned shoulders and a crease appeared between the masculine eyebrows as his eyes came to rest on the little scar at the base of her throat.

Magenta wished she'd worn something to hide it. That she hadn't left it to chance to get back inside the house unseen in her overwhelming need to feel free of any jewellery or other encumbrances.

Her throat worked nervously as she asked, 'Did you have a successful meeting?' She had presumed it was a meeting. Why else would he have shot off the way he had if something urgent hadn't cropped up?

'*Very* successful,' he emphasised. 'And fruitful.'

So why didn't he look happier? she wondered. He looked hot and dishevelled, as though he had been battling with every juggernaut that had dared to use his stretch of the motorway, and from the creases in his trousers he had been sitting in his car for a long time. Nevertheless, that didn't stop him from looking utterly desirable. So desirable that she had to look away, so that he wouldn't guess at the sudden tightening of her breasts and the almost-painful throb beneath the stretchy material of her dusky-pink cropped leggings.

'Why didn't you tell me you had suffered a cerebral haemorrhage?'

Magenta looked at him, startled, swallowing to ease the sudden dryness in her throat. 'You didn't ask.'

'I'm asking you now.'

When she didn't answer at once, he said with mounting impatience, 'Weren't we close enough in the past? Did you think it didn't matter, not bothering to acquaint me with that fact?'

Magenta looked at him askance, wishing he didn't look quite so amazing. 'Perhaps I didn't want you thinking I was inviting any false sympathy from you.'

Incredulity leapt in his eyes, and now she could see how pale his skin looked despite being bathed by the early evening sun.

'You really put me down as being that indifferent?' He tossed his jacket down on the seat. 'And thought that I wouldn't feel as shocked and rebuffed by your omission as I feel after finding out, as I have now?'

'Why?' Why did it matter to him? she thought. 'Why would it even concern you? Unless you think it's likely to affect the way I do my job?'

'Don't put words in my mouth,' he advised.

His tone assured her he was in no mood for accusations or evasion tactics. Nevertheless she had to ask, 'Could I ask who told you?'

'One of the referees whose name you gave us. It seems he thought you were a remarkably efficient and pleasant-mannered receptionist at his legal practice, but he wondered if, because of the odd bout of things slipping your memory after what you'd suffered, you'd be capable of handling the position of a full-blown PA.'

'Well, of all the nerve...' Frustrated tears burned the backs of Magenta's eyes. 'The only thing I ever forgot was to jot down his dental appointment! And I misplaced a file once or twice. But everybody does that! And he *knew* my memory loss was only confined to things that happened for a spell immediately prior to...what happened to me,' she finished hesitantly, as though she didn't want to spell it out.

'So why didn't you mention it when you were interviewed by my colleagues?' Andreas enquired. 'Or at least tell me?'

'For that very reason,' Magenta admitted with a grimace. 'When people find out I've had a brain haemorrhage they tend to treat me as though I'm somehow inadequate. Less of a human being. They can't seem to help it. During the first couple of years after it happened I had to rely on total strangers to help me understand how to use a cash machine, or ask them to walk into the supermarket with me because I didn't have the confidence to try and find the entrance on my own. Some would help, but others would veer off as fast as they could—like I was an imbecile, or a danger to them or something. It was no use telling them that I'd once been as *normal* as they considered themselves to be, and that what happened to me could happen to anyone, regardless of age or nationality or intelligence.

'Some of that discrimination hasn't ended, even though I'm managing to raise a son, am back to jogging three miles round the block twice a week and have got myself a distinction in Business Studies. I found out that telling prospective employers about what had happened to me wasn't going to get me the sort of job that would pay the bills. In fact quite the reverse. You'd be surprised how many interviewers who seemed disposed to take me on suddenly turned off as soon as I explained why there was such a gap in my working life. By the time I got an interview with your company I'd already decided I wasn't going to mention it any more. It was easier just to say I'd taken a break because I was bringing up my son.

'But, yes, I had a cerebral haemorrhage. And, yes, it affected me drastically. I mean *all* my physical and some of my mental abilities for a while. But I was determined to recover. *Really* recover. I've been told I'm one of the lucky ones who do. So now you know the truth you can exercise the right I'm sure you must have as an employer and fire me for taking this job under false pretences.'

'What I'm going to do,' he said, in a lowered tone that

nevertheless revealed how shocked he still was, 'is sit down here...'

Pushing his jacket aside, his imperious hand was pulling her with him down onto the lovers' seat.

'And you're going to tell me everything. Everything you've omitted to tell me since I saw you in that wine bar. That is everything you can remember,' he appended, when they were sitting together beneath the creamy-pink flowers of the climbing honeysuckle. 'When did it happen. exactly?'

The colour was returning to the hard bronze of his skin, but he was still looking grim. Magenta wondered if it was anger at being kept in the dark over something so important or genuine concern for her that was responsible for the deepening lines around his eyes and mouth.

'Soon after we...' *After we broke up.* She couldn't say it. Even though she knew that that was when it had been.

'What?'

She flinched at Andreas's shocked incredulity as he guessed what it was she had been about to say.

'How soon after?'

One bared shoulder lifted almost imperceptibly. 'A matter of months.'

'Months?' He was looking increasingly shocked, the furrow between his thick black brows deepening. 'Then you didn't ever have a modelling career?'

'Not really.' She feigned a little laugh. 'I know. Ironic, isn't it?' she said, and thought, *Especially when you practically accused me of neglecting my son because of it.*

'Were you still with Rushford?' he pressed, choosing to ignore her last remark. 'Is that the real reason he left you?'

She shook her head. 'We weren't together.' *And we never had been. Not like that,* she thought. She was certain of it, but she didn't tell Andreas any of that, as that would make things too complicated.

'I was with Mum, but she couldn't handle it—especially

with the doctors having to deliver Theo while I was still in a coma.'

'You were in a *coma?*'

She nodded.

'While you were pregnant?'

Magenta could almost see his brain working overtime.

'He must have been very premature.'

'He was.'

But not by as much as he was probably thinking, she decided. She couldn't tell him that her baby had been delivered a mere three weeks early, because then he might put two and two together and guess the boy was his. And although she knew she should tell him she couldn't summon up the courage to do it. She was too fearful of what he might say—and, even worse, try to do. Besides, she thought, as a further means of justifying her actions in keeping the knowledge of Theo's paternity from Andreas, he had suffered quite enough shocks for one day without adding any more.

'Anyway, Mum sent an SOS to Great-Aunt Josie. She and Mum hadn't been talking for as long as I could remember. I think Josie had dared to voice her opinion about Mum's drinking when I was quite small and Mum had told her she wasn't welcome in our lives any more. I know I missed her. Despite my memory problem—' she pulled a self-deprecating face '—I hadn't forgotten that. She came like a shot, to take Theo off Mum's hands and look after him until I was able to start doing it for myself. And she took care of me as well, when I was able to come home from the hospital.'

'A very special lady,' Andreas commented.

'Yes, she is.' Just the thought of her great-aunt's kindness filled her dark eyes with tears.

'And you made it,' he remarked, smiling, his voice sounding oddly thickened.

'Yes, I made it.' *Even if* we *didn't,* she thought, with such an unexpected ache beneath her ribcage that she had to look away, breathing in the air that was heavily impregnated with the sweet scent of the honeysuckle until the moment passed.

'So you weren't kidding when you pretended…? Correction. When I thought you were pretending not to remember me, were you?' he asked unnecessarily. 'And today…when you went to pick up that book….'

She shook her head in confirmation.

'Do you really not remember what happened?'

She closed her eyes and shook her head. *Don't tell me, please,* she begged silently. She was becoming more and more convinced that she wouldn't like what the truth might reveal.

'Magenta.' He had slipped a hand under her hair, his touch so tender that involuntarily she turned her cheek into the stirring warmth of his palm. 'Magenta, look at me.' His voice was as gentle as his fingers.

Don't be kind, her mind pleaded with him. *I can't bear it if you're kind!*

He was only taking pity on her because of what he had just discovered, she realised, opening her eyes to a flash of scintillating colour as a kingfisher dived low over the brook. Its bright blue and orange plumage was almost fluorescent as it took off again with its glistening prize.

'However much your mind blanked me out, your body didn't, did it?' Andreas whispered, his mouth moving gently along the soft line of her jaw. 'You still remember this.' His lips were feather-light against the corner of her mouth. 'And this.' His mouth was but a hair's breadth above hers, teasing, toying with her, but not actually consummating the kiss.

She had forgotten Andreas's capacity for tenderness, but she remembered it now, feeling a surge of excruciating need building in her as his fingers played lightly along the smooth, yearning line of her throat.

A soft moan trembled on the air and she realised that it had come from her. She had no more defence against his particular brand of lovemaking than that little fish in the stream had had against its determined captor, she thought. But she didn't want to defend herself, or to resist him.

Knowing she was lost, she let her head drop back, her hair tumbling over his arm like a dark waterfall, while his thumb played over the small throbbing hollow at the base of her throat.

'Was this part of that time?' he breathed in a ragged whisper, bending his head again to press his lips against the jagged little white scar.

She nodded, reminded of the treatments and the surgery she had undergone to help her breathe—just to keep her alive—when the doctors had told her mother and her aunt that she probably wasn't going to make it. Against all the odds she had, and it had given her a different outlook—a totally new perspective—on life. But all that was a world away from this man, and this evening, and the scented warmth of these exquisite moments. She didn't want to dwell on anything that would spoil it for her.

When his mouth came down over hers she gave herself up to its demands, drowning beneath the kisses he had withheld. He was tugging her blouse down over her shoulders and she wriggled to get her arms free, bringing them up around his neck and clinging to him as though only his warm strength would sustain her.

As his hand closed over her breast and moulded her soft warmth to his palm, Andreas gave a deep groan of satisfaction.

Motherhood had made her breasts fuller, he noted appreciatively, letting his lips pursue the same path as his massaging hand. He heard her sharp gasp as his mouth closed over one dark-tipped nipple, and he smiled as he lifted his head to look at her.

She was lying across his arm with her eyes closed in total abandonment to her senses, the gentle curve of her forehead lined in rapturous agony, her long dark lashes splayed thickly against her cheeks. She was as enslaved by what he was doing to her as she had ever been, he realised gratifyingly, his hand measuring every soft curve and dip of the body that he knew so well and had long ago initiated as his.

He had mentally beaten himself up all the way back from his office because of what he had been thinking about her over the past few days. He had been ready to condemn her for a lifestyle of self-indulgence and self-seeking gratification when all the time she had undergone the worst physical, mental and emotional trauma it was possible for anyone to go through.

He had bellowed at his colleague when she'd asked if he thought Magenta was suitable to fill his PA's shoes, when really he had been bellowing at Magenta for not telling him— and at himself for the detrimental thoughts he had harboured about her.

He regretted them now with every shred of humanity he had in him, and although he had assured himself that he would never allow himself to get emotionally involved with her again, right at this moment he couldn't stop what was happening between them even if he wanted to.

'Let's go inside,' he whispered.

Those three little words broke through Magenta's sensual torpor, shocking her into realising what she was allowing to happen.

She was only here because he wanted to satisfy some warped sense of injustice. To get her to surrender to his mind-blowing ability to turn her on as no other man had ever turned her on. Really he had very little respect for her at all, and he would still despise her tomorrow.

'No...' It was a breathless protest as she struggled to sit up.

'What's wrong?' His face was a compilation of bewildered lines.

'I just don't want to do this...' Her own features were

pained, yet still flushed with the desire that had nearly allowed her to fling all her hard-won self-respect and dignity to the winds. But at least he allowed her her freedom.

'You could have fooled me.' He was looking at her as though she had just pulled a rug from under his feet. There were wings of colour across his cheeks and his eyelids were still heavy from the strength of his desire.

'I'm sorry. I got carried away. I thought I could, but I can't. We might have had something going six years ago,' she forced herself to say, with her agitated hands dealing with her blouse. 'But we both know it was purely sexual. At least it was for me.' It was taking all of her mental strength to reinforce what she had convinced him of—tried to convince herself of—all those years ago. 'And I don't go in for those kind of relationships any more.'

'How very commendable of you,' he said cynically.

'No, just realistic,' she corrected. 'A lot has happened since then. I have responsibilities now, and they have to come first.' Even though her body was still on fire from his love-play, and the thought of where that love-play could lead was driving her insane with wanting. 'I know it probably isn't the reason you gave me this job, but if you still want me working for you then we're going to have to keep things purely on a business level.'

A faintly mocking smile touched his mouth as he got up and stood looking down into her tense, rebellious features. 'You really think we can?'

The heaving muscles beneath his shirt assured her of just how much she affected him. His lids were heavy with the weight of his desire for her and there were slashes of deep colour infusing the taut skin across his cheeks.

He was right, Magenta thought. How was it ever going to be possible when their mutual chemistry was like two magnetic fields that splintered all reasoning and the most basic instincts of self-preservation, resisting anything in the way of their powerful and destructive collision?

But she had to resist whatever it was that made her so physically in tune with this man. Because if she allowed herself to get too close to him she would unequivocally wind up getting hurt. And, worse than that, on the way to her own self-imposed heartache she'd feel duty-bound to tell him the truth about her son. And if she did that, and he tried to hurt her by taking Theo away from her, she would never be able to bear it. No pain in the universe could ever be greater than that.

'I resisted death,' she reminded him, ignoring the way her body still ached for his touch. She had to drag herself away from him, and with her voice cracking from the effort as she started to move away she added hastily over her shoulder, 'It'll be a doddle resisting you.'

CHAPTER SIX

'IS THERE ANYTHING else you aren't telling me?' Andreas enquired from behind his desk the following morning.

'Like what?' Magenta responded, jolted out of her wild speculation as to what it might have been like if she'd wound up in bed with him yesterday to face his unexpected and startling question.

A broad shoulder lifted beneath an immaculate jacket. 'You tell me.'

The way Magenta's heart was racing was making her legs go weak. 'N-nothing you need to know,' she told him, slipping a folder back into its alphabetical place in the tall metal filing cabinet. Had he noticed the way her voice was shaking? She sincerely hoped he hadn't.

'Magenta, look at me,' he commanded softly.

He had said the same thing in the garden yesterday and it had nearly been her undoing. Nevertheless, after pushing the drawer closed on its runners, she did as he had asked.

'I think we should do something to help your memory,' he said, surprising her, because that wasn't what she had been expecting at all.

Her sidelong glance at him was wary. 'What do you have in mind?'

'Nothing specific.' He put down the pen with which he'd

been idly tapping his fingers. 'And certainly nothing like you're imagining.'

'You don't know what I'm imagining,' she countered, her mouth going dry.

'Don't I?'

He rose to his feet and came around the desk, starting warning bells clanging in Magenta's head.

He was going out this morning and was dressed to kill, and she couldn't keep her eyes off the superb lean lines of his physique, enhanced by the equally superb cut of a light beige suit.

'I told you last night,' she reminded him, thinking back to the conversation they had had over dinner, after that disconcerting episode in the garden. 'It's only specific things I don't seem to remember now, and even they are coming back...gradually.'

'Even so,' he maintained, 'I'd like my doctor to take a look at you. He's quite a specialist in the field of psychology.'

'You think my problem's psychological rather than physical?' she suggested, rather sceptically.

Andreas shrugged in a way that suggested he was keeping an open mind.

'I don't need a doctor,' Magenta argued. 'I've seen enough doctors to last me a lifetime and they've all said the same thing. That anything I haven't retrieved might not come back at all. If it's going to, then I have to be patient. That's all. As I said, things *have* started coming back....'

'That's good. But it isn't only your loss of memory that concerns me. You haven't been eating properly. You're passing out—'

'I passed out *once!*' she reminded him emphatically.

'Nevertheless, I think you've come close to it on more than one occasion, and it could happen again. Anywhere. Any time. On the underground. Walking downstairs. When you're crossing the street. And next time it could be when you're on your own.'

'No, it couldn't.'

'Oh?' He was frowning down at her from his superior height, an authoritative figure, in command of himself and everything around him. In fact everything she wasn't—or didn't feel as if she was just at that moment. 'What makes you so sure?'

Because it's only when I'm with you that I'm affected so drastically!

'Would you let me take you to see him?' he pressed, taking her last comment as a further obstruction to what he was suggesting. 'I've already checked and he has a free appointment late this afternoon.'

'If it makes you happy.' She conceded defeated. 'And only if it's a condition of my employment.'

The trace of a smile touched his lips. 'It is.'

So that was that, Magenta thought. Decision made.

'I told you it wasn't necessary,' she said, when they were walking down the tree-lined drive of the doctor's clinic much later that afternoon. Naturally it had been a private consultation, which had probably cost Andreas the earth.

'If you call being diagnosed with a clean bill of health—apart from a bit of expert advice on looking after yourself—unnecessary,' Andreas answered, his mouth pulling in a grimace as he handed her into the car, 'then I have to disagree with you.'

'Because now you know I'm fit enough to work for you, and you don't have to worry too much about curbing your need to have a go at me for my past misdemeanours whenever you feel like it. Is that it?'

'Right on both counts,' he agreed with a twitching of his mouth, before the passenger door clicked softly closed, securing her in his car's silent bubble of tasteful opulence.

Watching him moving around the gleaming bonnet, his commanding and superbly clad physique marking him as a man who was as rich and successful as the car he drove suggested, Magenta had the strongest suspicion that he wasn't talking about either of those things at all.

The next couple of days passed in a sort of fragile, unacknowledged truce.

Despite what he had said Andreas seemed to be going easy on her now that he had found out exactly what she had been through, and Magenta didn't feel the need to oppose or contradict him at the least opportunity.

On the other hand he wasn't actually doing anything to try and boost her memory either. Perhaps, she considered, he was doing as his doctor and all the other doctors she had seen since her collapse had advised, and allowing things to return naturally. Or perhaps he just wanted to dismiss that whole period of his life as too insignificant to waste any more time on, as he had been more than ready to assure her it was on more than one occasion.

She berated herself for the little twinge of pain she experienced just from thinking that might be the case, and forced herself to concentrate on her work.

Working alongside him, however, revealed just how dynamic a businessman he was as he plunged into his punishing work schedule with a driving energy that left Magenta breathless.

In turn she was kept busy herself—on the telephone, typing letters and conference notes, and generally being his right hand when he took her with him to his various meetings. It was harder and more challenging than any job she had done in her life, but she was delighted when she found herself rising to the challenge. She was even more delighted when he praised her ability.

She was convinced, though, that he was only going easy

on her because of what he had learned about her. For all her speculation about him wanting to forget the past she didn't doubt that her sexual capitulation was still on his mind, even if his need to verbally flay her had been tempered by what he now knew. He was still a healthy, virile man, who had made no qualms about wanting a woman who had once been unable to stop herself from showing just how much she wanted him. She only hoped that she could finish this assignment and leave with her pride intact before he called her bluff. Before he showed her that she *couldn't* resist his particular brand of persuasion, as she had so adamantly and stupidly dared to claim to be able to in the garden the other day, and she wound up exactly where he wanted her to be. Back in his bed.

And, because of the way her insides turned to mush every time he walked into a room where she happened to be, it wasn't just a case of *if* any more, but *when*.

'How are you getting on working in your rich man's mansion?' Aunt Josie asked matter-of-factly the following afternoon. 'Andreas, isn't it?'

Andreas had popped out for an hour, and Magenta had seen Mrs Cox leaving in her car for town with one of the maids at lunchtime. Consequently Magenta hadn't been able to resist telephoning her aunt to see how Theo was.

'He's rich, but he isn't mine,' she corrected, with an attempted little laugh.

'But you'd like him to be, wouldn't you?'

'What makes you say that?' Magenta asked, taken aback by the directness of the woman's question.

'I'm your great-aunt, yet you mean as much to me as if you were my own daughter. What is it, love? Something's bothering you, and it isn't just a hankering for a rich boss who sounds a bit too attractive for his own good.'

Steeling herself, Magenta said, 'I had a fling with him once. That's what's wrong. It was six years ago, and all mixed up in that period of my life that was wiped out after my brain haemorrhage. His doctor said I might have blanked it out subconsciously.'

'*His* doctor?' Josie Ashton noted. 'That sounds like this Andreas is a man with a mission.'

'Perhaps,' Magenta murmured, unable to explain to her aunt just what she thought Andreas Visconti's mission might be. 'But apparently his doctor's a bit of a specialist in the field. Anyway, things *are* coming back—although I still can't remember everything about what happened between Andreas and me. From things he's said, I don't think it ended very amicably, but one thing I do know...' Magenta hesitated, inhaling deeply before she went on to impart, 'Theo's *his,* Aunt Josie.'

There was a long pause at the end of the line before the disembodied voice replied, 'I guessed as much.'

'What do you mean?' Magenta asked. Her aunt was continuing to surprise her. 'How could you? Even Mum didn't know. I mean...she thought...she said...'

'She said that during the time you'd obviously conceived, which was just before that part of your life you've never been able to remember, you'd had several purely casual boyfriends.'

Magenta cringed at how she had ever allowed herself to be convinced of that, although her mother obviously believed it to be true.

'I know.' Josie Ashton let out a sigh. 'I've suspected that it was Andreas somebody-or-other for a long time—though your mother was under the impression he was no one special even when I raised the question with her as long ago as when you were in that hospital. But to me there's nothing casual about a man whose name is on a woman's lips when she's still drugged up, floating in and out of a coma.'

'Why didn't you ever say anything?' Magenta queried, amazed that she could even have spoken his name when, after regaining full consciousness, she hadn't remembered a thing about him until that night he'd walked into that bar.

'I did. Once or twice. After you came back to live with me when you came out of hospital. But you seemed to deny all knowledge of him, so I gave up asking after a while.'

And she probably didn't remember *that,* Magenta thought, because she'd been in a kind of daze, with her body still repairing itself, at the time.

'Have you told him?

Josie meant about Theo being Andrea's son.

'No.'

'But you're going to?'

It was more than a question coming down the line.

'I can't, Aunt Josie. Not yet.'

'Why ever not?' The woman's tone was incredulous. 'Doesn't the man have a right to know that he's fathered a child? Doesn't Theo have the right to know who his father is?'

'Of course he does. But I have to do it in my own time.' She could hear her son's eager little voice in the background, begging his aunt to let him have the phone. 'You won't say anything to him, will you?' Magenta begged, panicking. 'You won't tell him? Not until I can?' There was an almost desperate edge to her voice now. 'Promise you won't.'

'Of course I shan't tell him,' Aunt Josie placated her.

'What won't you tell me?' The little boy had obviously scrambled up on to the woman's lap, as he did with Magenta sometimes when she was on the phone, and was trying to reach the mouthpiece. 'What won't she tell me, Mummy?'

'Nothing, poppet.' Magenta's voice became gently protective. 'Now, more importantly, what have you been doing? Did you go riding this morning, as you said you were going to?'

It was with a suppressed sigh of relief that Magenta realised the little boy had forgotten all about his aunt's conversation with his mother, and was giving her a breathless account of how the little Shetland pony that the local farmer had said he could ride had been lame.

'Oh, darling, there'll be another time,' she consoled, hearing the disappointment in his voice. 'When you come home Mummy will see what she can do about sending you for lessons.'

A movement by the door brought her head whipping round. Andreas was leaning against the doorframe, listening to every word she was uttering!

'How—how long have you been standing there?' She sounded almost as breathless as the five-year-old she had forgotten about for a few seconds. 'Look, darling, I have to go. Mummy will call you later. Say bye-bye to Aunt Josie for me.'

She'd tossed down her phone before Andreas had had time to move.

'Why so jumpy?' He smiled as he moved away from the door. 'Do you think I'm the type of boss who's likely to extract payment for personal calls in office hours?'

When she didn't answer immediately, too disconcerted by just how much he might have heard, he came closer.

'Of course if that's what you were hoping...'

She didn't know how it happened, but suddenly he was leaning over her behind her chair, with one arm across her breasts, unleashing a riot of betraying sensations inside her as she felt his lips against the nape of her neck.

'Do you usually get your kicks out of listening in on other people's private conversations?' Her breath was coming raggedly and causing her breasts to rise with exquisite torture against his dark sleeve.

'Why? Were you saying something I wasn't supposed to hear?' He was lifting the collar of her white silky blouse away from her neck—devoid of any scarf today—and gently fanning the pale exposed skin with his breath.

Magenta visibly shuddered from the sensuous tingles that were running down her spine. 'Of course not.'

'Are you sure?'

Dear heaven! What was he saying? Doing to her?

She gave a soft moan as he dragged his hand across her burgeoning breasts.

'Have you ever wondered what it would be like to make love on a desk, Magenta? Or perhaps you've already tried it?'

'No, I haven't!' The fear of what he might have heard her saying was being replaced by another insidious fear, and that was being unable to resist giving in to this almost overwhelming and terrifying desire to succumb to him. 'Mrs Cox may come in.'

'Mrs Cox is off duty.' Long fingers deftly slipped the first button of her blouse.

'One of the maids, then.'

'Both off duty.' A smile laced his voice as he pushed the pale slippery fabric he'd loosened down over one silken shoulder. 'Isn't this making you remember? We almost made love on a table once, but unfortunately our…intentions were rather impeded.'

'*Your* intentions you probably mean.' It was a breathless accusation, and one threaded through with shuddering desire as his teeth grazed with arousing skill along her shoulder.

'Oh, no.' He laughed low in his throat. 'I never did anything without a willing accomplice. Don't you want to remember, Magenta, how sexy I said you looked draped in nothing but that tablecloth?'

The tablecloth! Slashes of colour rose before her eyes, but then the jumble of vivid images took very definite shape. It was red and white chequered linen, and its starched coarseness was an unbelievable turn-on against her painfully aroused breasts.

'You were afraid of being caught even then doing something you knew you shouldn't.'

She pressed her hands flat against her ears. 'I don't want to remember!' Her statement was one of negation and rising panic.

'Oh, I think you do.' He came around her chair, positioning

himself on the desk, so close that his bent knee was touching her arm. With a gentle firmness he pulled her hands down. 'A grabbed hour's privacy. We were desperate for each other. It was a Monday night and the restaurant was closed. We thought we were alone.'

But someone had come back... Magenta put her hand to her temple. 'Oh, dear heaven!' she groaned.

She could still hear the key in the lock—the door opening. Then voices—Giuseppe Visconti and a woman. Maria Visconti! It had been dark and they hadn't seen her! Had she really let Andreas undress her there at that discreet table at the back of the restaurant? How could she have let him?

She shook her head as other images raced in. Her panicking and Andreas whipping the cloth off the table and throwing it around her. He'd been still fully clothed. There had been a storeroom...no, a cupboard...which he'd hustled her into. She remembered standing there and keeping very quiet and still—trying not to move. And Andreas...Andreas having other ideas...

She closed her eyes, remembering the sensations that had fired through her when he had used that coarse cloth to arouse her. Moving it like a towel, slowly and calculatedly drawing it back and forth along her body in a deliberate and excruciatingly sensual attempt to see how long she could keep herself from breaking the silence with a moan of pleasure.

Had she really been a participant in that? Or was it all part of some hazy, sensuous dream? No wonder his family had thought her such a little tramp if they had guessed!

'You see,' she heard him say quietly above her. 'It's easy when you know how.'

Her eyes were troubled as they met his gaze and saw the faint light of awareness burning there. 'We didn't...do it there?' She had no memory of that.

'Not exactly.'

Because his determination to please her and drive her out

of her mind with wanting would have superseded even his own hot-blooded need for gratification. Because he was like that—and she had been his willing, subjugated toy!

'That wasn't me.' She groaned again, dropping her chin onto her bent hand and supporting it by her elbow on the desk. And, echoing her thoughts of a moment ago, 'No wonder they thought me so cheap. So easy.'

'I promise you no one ever found out.'

She sent a glance up at him. 'Didn't they miss that tablecloth?'

'I was responsible for setting up the tables for the following day's lunch. It was easy to let them think I'd simply overlooked it.'

'And you?' She leaned back, her arms dropping resignedly onto the padded arms of her chair. 'What did you think of me?'

'You drove me mad,' he admitted with a self-deprecating grimace.

'And because of the way I behaved with you, you imagine I behave in the same abandoned fashion with every man I meet, that I'd be just as willing to jump into bed with you again now?'

His eyebrow lifted, but he made no comment on that score. 'Stop feeling so bad about it,' he advised instead. 'We were young and hungry for each other.' Tilting her face to his with the crook of his finger, he leaned forward and lightly kissed her on the mouth. 'There were two of us in that cupboard that night,' he reminded her softly. 'But I'm more inclined to reserve the bedroom for making love these days, and I can certainly assure you that I would treat you with much more consideration now.'

But not respect.

He didn't even need to say it.

'Beautiful Magi...'

The caressing stroke of his hand along her throat brought

her eyelids down against his unbearable tenderness. His eyes, when she opened hers again, were two sapphire pools of unfathomable emotion as they raked mercilessly over her tortured face.

'I think that's enough recall therapy for one day, don't you?' he advocated, his hand falling away from her. And, getting up from the desk, he picked up some letters she had typed for him which were lying in her tray and casually took himself off to his own room.

Andreas had arranged to attend a business dinner that Friday, although it hadn't been marked in his diary and Magenta didn't find out about it until the actual day arrived.

'I'm sorry to spring this on you at such short notice,' Andreas expressed, coming into her office looking unusually rushed, his jacket hooked over his shoulder, only hours before the planned event. 'I don't suppose you brought anything dressier with you than suits and blouses?'

'Leggings and trainers?' she quipped. Guessing from the sudden frown knitting his dark brows that he wasn't in the mood for wisecracks, she went on, 'I didn't realise that my first week as your PA would call for dressing up for a night out at The Ritz.' She shrugged. 'Or wherever,' she added, not even certain yet where he was supposed to be going. 'I'm sorry. I imagined I'd be going home tonight.'

'Did you?' he breathed, in a way that made her wish that she hadn't. 'As you've already stated, you're my PA. That means you're on call twenty-four-seven. Is that clear?' When she nodded rather uncertainly, he said, with his keen eyes assessing her, 'Was there anything important you had planned?'

'No, but—'

'In that case we'd better get you something.'

We? Magenta darted a questioning glance up at him. He was already shrugging into his jacket.

'I'm sure I could probably find something in my wardrobe at home if you could spare me for a few hours.'

'I can't.'

Which was just as well, Magenta decided. She doubted that she had anything suitable for the type of venue to which he'd be taking her. She hadn't had much call to wear cocktail dresses since she'd had Theo—even if she'd been able to afford them.

'You're going to have to give me a sub on my salary,' she told him worriedly when they arrived at a busy village with upmarket little shops. She was already paying the maximum amount she could off her credit card, which she used to cover household essentials, and she had nowhere near sufficient funds in her bank account to cover her bills, let alone spend on dresses.

Andreas didn't respond as he pulled into a well-maintained car park.

'Come on. Let's get you kitted out,' he said a few minutes later, taking her hand.

The only dress shop in the village, Magenta realised, was an exclusive bow-windowed boutique. The type of place that looked as though it would stock just one of each luxuriously designed item displayed in its minimally dressed window.

'They must have known you were coming.' Andreas pulled a wry face. 'That dress was obviously made for you. Didn't blue used to be your favourite colour?'

It still was, Magenta thought distractedly, gazing up at the chic, exquisitely tailored dress in the window.

A sleeveless little number in royal blue silk, in a wraparound design that moulded itself beautifully to a slender figure, the dress had a plunging neckline that was low enough to be alluring without being immodest, and a hemline that was cut just above the knee. It was tied with a side-fastening sash that emphasised the waist and the bustline, and the long, loose ends of the sash fell freely against the flatteringly curved skirt.

'You have to be joking, don't you?' Magenta felt wounded anger welling up inside her. 'You *know* this sort of thing is way out of my league. I wouldn't have a thing to wear with it even if I could afford it—which I can't!'

A silver clutch bag and a silver and blue sequinned stole draped over a marble pedestal spoke of elegance in the extreme, while on another lower pedestal a pair of silver high-heeled sandals looked like something even Cinderella would have thought twice about losing. Pinpricks of small blue stones graced the sides of straps which were little more than silver strands across the ankles, so elegant they might have been real sapphires. They probably were, Magenta thought, if the fact that nothing in the window carried a price tag was anything to go by!

'I would have thought it wouldn't have taken much working out for you to realise that High Street is more within my budget.' Ridiculously, she was fighting back tears as she made to swing away.

What she didn't expect was to feel Andreas's firm hands upon her shoulders.

'Think of it as a business expense,' he drawled, and before she had time to argue he was hustling her into the shop. In response to the incredulous upward glance she shot him, he added, 'There *are* some perks to being at my beck and call.'

Evidently there were, Magenta agreed mentally as she tried on the dress in the scented changing room at the back of the shop. The shop owner had had to take it off the model, as the only similar one by the same designer had been too large. But this one, she realised with a lick of pleasure running through her, was a perfect fit.

'Do you think these shoes will look all right with this?' she asked Andreas when she came out of the changing room.

She was frowning down at the dainty low-heeled black sandals she wore every day.

He had been talking to the owner, a rather glamorous, middle-aged woman, who was smiling at Magenta from behind the counter. Now, as he turned and saw her standing there, he gave a low whistle under his breath.

He looked totally taken aback—unable to speak. But then he seemed to give himself a mental shake before glancing down at her very inappropriate footwear.

'Doesn't she look beautiful?' the shop owner enthused.

'Exquisite.'

Andreas couldn't seem to take his eyes off her, Magenta noticed with warm sensations infiltrating her blood, and for a few moments it felt as though there were only the two of them in the shop.

But he had totally forgotten what she had asked him! she realised, when he turned away towards the counter again and she saw him reaching into the top pocket of his jacket for his wallet.

'How much for the window?'

She couldn't believe what he had just asked, but the woman was jotting something down on a piece of paper, and after a nod from him started bustling around like a bee that had just scented a rare and beautiful pollen—which somehow indicated that Magenta *had* heard correctly.

'You can't,' she whispered behind his broad back, when the woman had moved into the window area to claim the shoes and bag and the matching stole.

'Go back to the changing room,' he said without looking at her as he took a credit card out of his wallet.

As she didn't feel like protesting in front of an audience, Magenta could only comply.

She didn't know if the shoes the woman brought her were the ones in the window, or if there had been another pair in her size, but the ones that had been handed round the heavy velvet curtain for her to try fitted her like hand-made gloves.

Or glass slippers, she thought wryly, remembering what she had been thinking outside.

Their purchases were being lovingly wrapped in tissue paper when Magenta emerged from the changing room in her suit and blouse. Andreas pulled a wry face at her transformation from virtual sex kitten to businesswoman as he slipped his credit card back into his wallet.

The clutch-bag was the last purchase to be wrapped, and Magenta spied a trio of minute sapphire stones winking up at her from the flap of soft silvery leather before they too disappeared within folds of rustling tissue paper.

'Your girlfriend's a very lucky lady.' The shop owner was silently admiring the tall man she had been addressing, although it was Magenta that her smile alighted on.

I'm not his girlfriend! she wanted to stress, but that would have made her sound as if she were something altogether more eyebrow-raising, so she just smiled and took the bunch of glossy carrier bags the woman handed her with good grace.

'I can't believe you just did that,' she remarked, flabbergasted, as soon as they were outside, walking away from the shop. 'You've just spent a fortune on something I may only ever wear once.'

His long strides were marking out their purposeful path to the car park. 'Is that all you have to say?'

'What do you expect me to say?' she uttered, still totally dumbfounded. She had to quicken her stride to keep up with him.

'A simple thank you would suffice.'

Of course. If his motive was merely to see her properly attired for a business dinner then she was behaving crassly and with total ingratitude. She was about to apologise and thank him, as he'd suggested, but the simple words he'd spoken were suddenly echoing back at her from out of the dark recesses of her mind.

A simple thank you would have sufficed.

She stopped at the end of the little row of shops, her hand going automatically to her forehead.

'What is it? What's wrong?'

Andreas's concern broke through the wild confusion of her thoughts.

'I thought…I just thought you'd said something like that to me before.' She shook her head as shapes started to form out of the mists of that lost time. 'It was that statue….'

A little porcelain statue of a mother and her child, a girl of about three or four, who was holding her hand and looking up trustingly at the woman. She'd seen it in a shop window and had wanted it for her mother, to try and cheer her up after another of her endless break-ups. To try and stop her drinking and let her know that she had so much else to live for. To let her know how much her daughter really loved her. Needed her…

'I went back to the shop and it was gone…' Her brow furrowed with the aching disappointment that seemed to have gripped her insides. 'What is it they say? The first time we remember something we actually relive it all over again? And the second time we think of it it's only a memory?'

'Discontinued,' the assistant had told her when she had asked if he had another, and it had felt like the end of the world. She couldn't believe how badly she had wanted that statue and how the anguish at losing it could have been so bad.

'You asked me why I was crying…' She looked up at Andreas. She remembered that when she had told him he had rung around shop after shop, trying to find another. And when he had he'd made an eighty-mile round trip in his father's van just to pick it up for her. 'You found one for me.'

She remembered showering him with kisses. Laughing and crying right there in the reception area of the pokey little solicitors' office where she'd worked. She could see him laughing. Looking amused. And, yes…he had said those words to her then: 'A simple thank you would have sufficed.'

His arm was around her now, warm and supportive, and without thinking Magenta leaned in to his steadying strength.

His shoulder felt like a rock beneath her trembling cheek, and for a few moments it didn't matter that they were in a village high street congested with local traffic. That there were Friday afternoon shoppers milling around the place and harassed mothers calling errant youngsters energised by the freedom of their summer holiday.

'Oh, Andreas! What happened to us?' she appealed to him.

'Not here. Not yet.' Determinedly he took her hand and guided her across the busy street. 'Perhaps not anywhere.' His voice had a strange quality to it as they reached the entrance to the car park on the other side of the road. 'Perhaps it's best forgotten,' he said.

CHAPTER SEVEN

THE DINNER THAT evening, attended by some of the biggest names in the UK hotel business, was held in the ballroom of an impressive nineteenth-century stately home, somewhere deep in the heart of the Surrey countryside.

Andreas had informed Magenta that he'd been in two minds about going, which explained why it hadn't been entered into his diary, but then he had heard that among those attending there would be two of his acquaintances from the States whom he was very keen to see. They were over here, he had explained, to sell their shares in some of the country house hotel properties they owned in the UK, and as it was a section of the market he was keen to move into he felt it would be beneficial for him to be there with his PA.

It was the first formal event Magenta could remember attending, although she knew from photographs she'd seen of herself that she'd attended one or two with Marcus Rushford during the early days of her short-lived modelling career. It was with a little shiver of nerves, therefore, that she viewed the long, beautifully laid tables, taking in with some trepidation the spectacle of sparkling crystal and gleaming silverware beneath the luminescence of two glittering chandeliers. Then she felt Andreas's supporting hand at her elbow, followed by a few, soft encouraging words, and she wondered if he'd guessed how she was feeling as he led her into the breathtaking room.

A few hours later, sipping her second cup of coffee, with the speeches and most of the business of the evening well out of the way, Magenta couldn't understand why she had been so nervous. The Ottermans were lovely, as it turned out.

PJ, as Andreas had introduced him, was a short, greying-haired man, with a ginger moustache and a warm, infectious laugh. His wife, Mary-Louise, was an elegant, quietly-spoken lady who, from her clear skin and slender figure, had clearly taken care of herself. She was, however, temporarily confined to a wheelchair, with her leg in plaster, as a result of a fall over an unattended suitcase at the airport on her arrival in the UK the previous week.

'That's such an unfortunate thing to happen,' Magenta sympathised when Mary-Louise made reference to her ill-timed accident. 'Especially with the weather being so beautiful here at the moment and you having to forgo all the organised walks you and your husband were planning for this trip.'

'Yes, I suppose it has been a bit careless of me,' the woman admitted with a self-effacing grimace. 'But secretly, my dear...' Her slim shoulders hunched, she leaned towards Magenta with a conspiratorial lowering of her voice '...I'm rather enjoying having PJ fussing over me in a way that he hasn't done in forty years.'

Magenta laughed, enjoying the American woman's company while Andreas was talking business to the woman's husband. Both men were on their feet, as they had been for some time now, and Magenta was very conscious of Andreas standing behind her chair.

If she leaned back she could touch him...

She was careful not to, however, because she had done so already, when she'd tilted her head back in response to something someone had been saying about the chandelier

earlier and her hair had brushed the impeccable dark sleeve
of his dnner jacket.

Mary-Louise was saying something about the London Eye,
and shamefully Magenta found herself having to try and tune
in to listen when really she wanted to hang on to every word
that deep, masculine voice behind her was uttering. To breathe
in the intoxicating scent of the cologne he was wearing and
try and deal with the sensations that having him standing
there so close and yet so oblivious to her produced.

'I haven't been on it,' Magenta confessed, reproaching herself for allowing her attention to stray from what her easy and
genteel dinner companion was saying. 'I'm afraid I'm not the
world's best contender when it comes to heights, but I'm—'

Her sentence was cut short when two over-animated
young men in evening suits, beer mugs in hand, barged past
Mary-Louise as though there was no one sitting there. At
her small shocked gasp Magenta was appalled to notice that
there were splashes of beer spilled down the sleeve of the
woman's blouse.

'Here! Let me.' Magenta was on her feet and mopping up
the liquid that was dripping off the chair with her napkin,
while Mary-Louise dabbed at her blouse with her own.

'Are you all right?' Andreas and PJ spoke in unison, their
business discussion discarded by their concern.

'Yes, yes—I'm fine,' the woman uttered quickly, clearly
not wanting to draw more attention to herself than was absolutely necessary. But Magenta was quietly annoyed.

Having assured Mary-Louise that her blouse hadn't suffered too much, Magenta noticed that the two men who had
bumped into the chair had not only stopped to share a loud
joke with two other young men just a few metres away, but
that one of them actually had the gall to be sizing her up.

'Just because she's in a wheelchair it doesn't mean that
she's invisible.' The reprimand slipped out before she could
stop it.

'I'm sorry.' One of the lads mouthed an apology and, look-ing shamefaced now, barged hastily through another group of people who were standing by a nearby table, with his three friends hot on his heels.

Andreas had been aware all evening of the growing rapport between Magenta and Mary-Louise. Now, observing them while conversing with PJ, he noticed the older woman close her weathered hand affectionately over Magenta's and heard her say, 'That was very sweet of you.'

With a sudden sharp kick of something in his loins he wished that *he* could be the one touching Magenta right then. The way she had stood up for his friend's wife had impressed him immeasurably. He guessed that it sprang from her own first-hand experience of other people's thoughtlessness at a time when she had been less than able-bodied herself.

He noticed, too, how easily the Ottermans, particularly Mary-Louise, had taken to her. People always had, he re-alised, despite her own claim to not forming many friend-ships. At nineteen she had had a warm and open spontaneity. He remembered how she had used it—effortlessly and unconsciously—to try and win over his grandmother. Maria Visconti, however, had refused to warm to her.

PJ and Mary-Louise were having no such reservations. With an unnecessary twinge of irritation Andreas caught their laughter at something Magenta had just said to them. She was sitting down again, and PJ had taken the seat he him-self had been sitting in, his arm across the back of her chair.

She was wearing that glorious hair up, with soft tendrils fanning her face. He had a strong desire to delve his hands deeply into it, to hear the pleasured gasps from the dark bur-gundy of her tantalising mouth. The way that beautiful blue dress parted as she crossed her legs gave him an alluring glimpse of one silkily sheathed thigh. In fact the whole dress was driving him virtually insane with the need to feel her against him, and he knew he had to satisfy that need very soon or go mad.

'If you'll excuse us…?' He cut across something PJ was saying and caught her hand. 'Well?' he said to her, his body so rigid from battling to contain his arousal that it was an effort to smile. 'Are you going to show me what you can do?'

He sensed her recoil almost imperceptibly, as she had when she'd accidentally touched him earlier.

She smiled a little awkwardly. 'I think I'd rather sit this one out.'

Her glance towards Mary-Louise suggested that she might not want to dance because the other woman couldn't. He'd already heard Mary-Louise telling her when the music started how much she'd always loved to dance. Or maybe Magenta had another reason for refusing him, he thought. Maybe she just didn't trust herself to be that close to him…

'Nonsense, my dear.' The woman gave Magenta's hand a reassuring pat. 'Don't refuse on my account. You young people need a minute to yourselves.'

From the way she had been looking at himself and Magenta during the evening it was pretty obvious that she knew there was something more to their relationship than just business.

'And I can assure you that I'll be up there tripping the light fantastic before the next six months are up—although perhaps not to something with quite so much angst.'

Pretending to laugh with the others did nothing to relax Magenta as Andreas led her onto the dance floor.

'It looks like you were out-voted, doesn't it?' he mocked softly above the fluid notes of a first-rate female ballad singer.

He looked quite smug. As well he might, Magenta decided, having no choice but to follow him into the midst of the swaying bodies.

'I was just being considerate, that's all,' she bluffed as he turned her around and his arms came round her.

'Very commendable.' His smile was devastating. 'Now be considerate towards *me*.'

A shocked little gasp escaped her as his body made contact with hers. Never had she felt so naked dancing with a man in public. His hard warmth was penetrating the fine silk of her dress as if she were wearing nothing, and the sensuous cloth of his dinner jacket made her want to press herself against him.

'It feels good.'

He was referring to the dress, and Magenta felt his hand sliding down her spine before it stopped just short enough to observe the rules of decency, its heat searing through the blue fabric just above the gentle swell of her buttocks.

'Isn't that why you bought it?'

He gave a disapproving click of his tongue. 'Would you believe me if I say I didn't know there would be dancing here tonight? It wasn't mentioned.'

'But now that there is you'll take full advantage of the fact?'

'Can you blame me? Especially when I'm aware of how much you want me to.'

'That's not true.' She turned her head away so that she couldn't see the mockery in his face—and wished she hadn't when he took the opportunity to pull her even closer. She sucked in a breath, feeling *his* breath—warm and erotic—fan the sensitive skin at her hairline.

'You're a poor liar, Magenta. I can feel the way your body's responding to me now, and it isn't the response of a woman who wants me to leave her alone.'

'But you're going to.' It was a desperate little command rather than a question.

'Until you're begging me otherwise.'

She could tell he was smiling. A slow, sexy smile.

'Verbally, of course.'

His words mocked. But then he could tell from the tension in her body how much she wanted him physically. Her breasts were aching for his caresses and her thighs were tingling above the sheer Lycra of her stockings, sending vibes of raw wanting to the heart of her femininity every time they collided with the hard-muscled strength of his.

Tilting her head back so that she was looking directly up into his incredibly charismatic features, she said huskily, and in a voice that was unintentionally provocative, 'Did this kind of fascinating technique turn me on before?'

His smile was discerning. 'It's working now, isn't it?'

She uttered a shrill little laugh. 'Were you always this conceited?'

'I call it being one step ahead of the game.'

His gaze dropped to her mouth, sending little tremors of excitement through her.

'And I don't believe you've forgotten quite as much as you claim.'

'Well, that's your opinion,' she breathed, and didn't tell him that there were more and more pieces of her memory that she was beginning to link together. That it had begun to scare her, and that she was almost terrified of what those still-lost pieces might eventually reveal.

'What is it?' Andreas asked over the female singer's sobbing finale of a story about a woman tortured by love. 'Am I probing too close to the truth? Or are you having another of your recall moments?'

'No... I...' Why did he have to be so astute? So totally 'ahead of the game', as he had just claimed to be?

Someone jostled her elbow and Andreas's arm tightened around her. The steadying action brought her up against his hard, lean length, so achingly close to him that her head began to swim and primitive impulses sent a throbbing awareness trembling through her body.

'Why don't we go home?' His words were a sensual caress against the shining bounty of her hair.

When she didn't reply, too afraid of what she might say if she did, she found herself allowing him to lead her away from the dance floor.

She didn't know what he was going to say to his friends, but they were back at their table and he was offering the Ottermans his apologies, extending an invitation for them to come and stay at the house before they returned to the States. His manner was easy and charming, without any need for explanation and without any artifice or awkwardness in his deep tones.

As they were walking out through the luxuriously carpeted foyer, past a round central table containing a huge floral display, Magenta couldn't even remember saying her goodbyes. All she seemed able to focus on was Andreas's arm around her shoulders and the need that was escalating inside her with each collision of his hard hip with hers.

It was going to happen, she thought. Despite all she had said and all the objections she had raised she was going to bed with Andreas Visconti again. And she couldn't decide how she had managed to come this far in just a few short days.

She couldn't stop it now even if she wanted to, she realised, with her arm slipping automatically beneath his jacket and around his lean waist.

The heat of his body through the fine shirt was a turn-on in itself. Her fingers ached to pull at the expensive silk, just as her body was aching to be closer to him—close enough to feel his burning flesh pulsing against hers.

Weak with wanting, she was counting the seconds until they reached the warm, dark privacy of his car.

'Andreas! Andreas Visconti!'

A man who had been passing them had stopped and was walking towards them now. He had cropped, receding brown hair and looked a few years older than Andreas.

'What has it been now?' He was extending a hand to him. 'Five years? No, more than that. Six years?

Magenta felt the loss of Andreas's arm around her shoulders as he shook hands with the man who, from his formal clothes, was obviously also attending the function. Apparently he was called Gerard, Magenta learned when she was introduced to him, and he'd used to be an assistant chef in Giuseppe Visconti's restaurant. Now he had shares in a small hotel in Brighton.

'I was sorry about your father,' he was saying to Andreas. 'It all happened so suddenly. But I've heard *you're* doing all right.' With his rather too-generous midriff, and a waistband that looked uncomfortably tight, the man was regarding Andreas with unconcealed envy. As though he wanted a taste of all that wealth and success that seemed to ooze from the tall, immaculately attired man he couldn't even begin to emulate. He glanced at Magenta, adding, 'And in more ways than one.'

Feeling the stranger's eyes drifting over her body, Magenta drew the sequinned wrap more closely around her. She had a feeling she might have known him, but the vibes that she was getting, which were putting her on her guard, suggested that if she had then the experience hadn't been a pleasant one.

'I must say I'm pleased to see the two of you back together again.' Those wandering eyes were taking more notice of Magenta now than of Andreas. 'I always thought it was a tragedy, your letting this lovely girl go.' He used 'this' as an excuse to let a rather podgy finger brush her shoulder.

'I didn't realise you were aware that Magenta and I were ever an item.' Andreas's voice had turned decidedly cold.

'I think we all were.' The man gave Magenta a rather knowing wink. 'There wasn't a man working in that kitchen or out front when I was there who didn't envy you, old chap. In fact I was thinking of making a play for her myself when I heard you'd split up. But then your father died. The restaurant closed...' He made an expressive gesture with his arms, the action pulling at the fabric already straining across his middle. 'I was out of a job, and *this* beautiful creature had already grabbed the attention of someone far smarter and richer than the likes of you and me.'

She didn't even need to ask to know that he was talking about Marcus Rushford.

Beside her, Magenta sensed the hostility building in Andreas towards his late father's employee. Hostility and an anger so palpable it was unnerving—although outwardly he appeared rigidly in control.

'Well, it's been a pleasure seeing you again, Gerard.' Magenta could almost hear those strong white teeth grinding together. 'But, as you can see, we're in a hurry.' And with a 'goodnight' that sounded more like a growl he was urging her out into the darkness of the car park.

Soft lighting around the building showed off the gleaming metalwork of the Mercedes as they approached it. It also showed Andreas's face, slashed with shadows and looking like a grim mask, as he pointed the remote control at the car as though it were something living he wanted to kill.

'Did that guy ever make his intentions towards you known when we—?'

He broke off, and from his exasperated sigh she knew he thought it was pointless even asking her. But she was well aware of what he had been going to say.

'He made a pass at me.' She remembered aloud as soon as they were in the car.

'What?' He looked as though it was Gerard he wanted to kill now. 'When? Where?'

'I don't know!' She dropped her head back against the rest. 'I only know he did.'

'And did you welcome it?'

She looked at him aghast as he started the engine. 'You're joking, surely?'

The glance he shot her was insultingly sceptical.

'Yeah, sure. I *loved* it!' she breathed.

He pulled out of the car park with an unnecessary squeal

of brakes, his features hard and rigid. His shirt showed up starkly white in the darkness.

He was angry because Gerard had brought up her involvement with Marcus Rushford, unaware of the damage it would do. Or perhaps he had been aware, she thought. Andreas had already accused her of virtually selling herself to the wealthy tycoon. But *had* she? Her nails dug into her palms as she struggled to remember. She couldn't have. How could she when she hadn't even wanted him in that way?

'Gerard made a pass at me,' she reiterated, trying to make it sound as though it was trivial. Unimportant. But the images manifesting themselves now were ones of sick revulsion. 'Men did. *Do.* I can't help it.'

'Neither can they.' His censorious glance across the emotion-charged space between them had her pulling the skirt of her dress over a suddenly far too exposed thigh.

'So what are you going to do? Lock me up and throw away the key?' When he didn't answer, too involved with dimming his lights as another car passed on the other side of the country road, she breathed, 'That's possessiveness, Andreas.'

Was that what had broken them up? Had she felt stifled by a relationship that was too intense to cope with? Or was it simply, as she'd wondered all along, that he had resented the fact she had wanted a career?

'If it is, then I can hardly be blamed for it, can I?' he rasped, flooding the road with angry light again.

'Why? Because I look the way I do? *You* virtually dressed me today, remember? And you aren't exactly the type of man the opposite sex can ignore.'

'Is that your way of reminding me of where we were an hour ago?'

Was it?

'No,' she refuted quickly, because it would be far too easy to rekindle the mood that had propelled them out of that hotel ballroom, and she'd known it was crazy even *thinking* of allowing herself to become intimately involved with him even before they had bumped into Gerard.

'As you wish,' he accepted, with a long drawing out of his breath, and he didn't say another word to her for the rest of the journey home.

CHAPTER EIGHT

'DO YOU WANT a nightcap?'

Andreas had removed his jacket, and his bow-tie was hanging loosely below the winged collar he had unfastened.

'No.' Magenta was much too conscious of being with him, knowing that if it hadn't been for meeting that man Gerard in the foyer they would have been in bed, making unrestrained love to each other now. 'I think I'd like to go up and maybe read for a while. Would it be imprudent of me in any way to ask if you would lend me the Byron?'

He glanced up from the sideboard, where he was pouring himself a drink. 'Still the incurable romantic?' When she didn't answer, not sure whether he was being sarcastic or not, he said, 'I suspect that you've already guessed—or remembered—that it's yours anyway.'

She nodded, wanting to ask why, if that was the case, he had it in his possession. But the moment didn't seem right somehow.

'Go in and get it,' he acceded, turning away.

Bidding him goodnight, she walked upstairs on legs of lead, her stole and her bag clutched tensely in her hand. She wanted him and he despised her. And he probably despised himself for wanting *her* too. That was probably why he had reined in those ravaging desires of his after he had been reminded of the kind of woman he obviously believed she was.

But she couldn't have been that loose or free, with other lovers in her past, could she? Not Marcus. Not anyone! There had only ever been Andreas. She knew it in her heart as surely as she knew that day would follow night into eternity.

The book was where she had left it when she had crept up there alone the other day—back in its place between a tome of classic literature and a Winston Churchill biography.

Trying not to look at the enormous bed, she tripped lightly across the room with her mind anywhere but on poetry, fighting back the feelings that were stirring in her as she pictured herself lying naked with Andreas under the folds of that abstract-patterned king-size duvet.

Putting her bag and stole down on a Jacobean-style chest, she was quickly retrieving the book when the light she'd switched on suddenly faded almost to candlelight.

Pivoting round, she saw Andreas coming around the door. 'Still here?'

Standing there with her lips slightly parted in shock, and with reckless impulses suddenly leaping through her, Magenta wasn't sure whether he was surprised or not.

She made a careless gesture towards the book. 'So it would seem.' Her throat had contracted so much she could scarcely get the words out as she watched him, his smile distracted, advance across the luxurious carpet towards her.

Somewhere between the sitting room and the bedroom he had unfastened most of the buttons of his shirt, and Magenta was acutely aware of the hair-sprinkled chest it exposed. He was so close to her now that she could reach out and touch him. But she didn't. Instead she stayed exactly where she was, riveted by his nearness, his scent and that powerful magnetism that made her protest to herself go unheard and kept her eyes trained painfully on his.

With the briefest touch of a finger he lifted her face to his, and then with a tenderness that was excruciating brought his mouth down over hers.

Magenta's senses screamed from the lightness of his touch, the calculated skill with which he was arousing her. Or *was* it calculated? she wondered. Perhaps he was merely kissing her goodnight.

She wanted to strain against him. Put her arms around his neck and cling to him. But the not knowing kept her still, her fingers almost painfully stiff around the velvety cover of the book.

'So where do we go from here?' His eyes were half veiled by his long lashes so that she couldn't tell what he was thinking. She knew her own eyes would be dark pools of wanting, so why did he need to ask?

But he was leaving it to her.

Candidly then, her face racked with longing, she murmured softly, 'I don't want to be alone.'

Without a word he moved across to the door he'd left open and closed it. That penetrating gaze never left hers as he came back to where she stood, tense with anticipation. A hot and heightening excitement was licking through her blood. She was breathing shallowly. Her eyes were slumberous with desire, their pupils dilated, the dark chocolate irises showing him the depths of her need.

He glanced down at the book she was still clutching and, taking it from her trembling fingers, laid it aside on the chest. Then he lifted a hand to remove the pins from her hair while her greedy senses soaked up his warmth and his hard dark strength, the stirring musk of his skin beneath his cologne.

Her hair tumbled down about her shoulders like a cascade of dark silk and she sucked in a breath as he dealt with the twist of silver she wore around her throat.

He put it to one side with the pins and the book, those blue eyes scarcely leaving hers for a second before his dark head bowed in studied concentration as he returned to the task in hand. With sure and calculated fingers he tugged at the knot at her waist and the dress fell open in easy compliance with his bidding.

Magenta pressed her eyes closed, her trembling lashes and the irregularity of her breathing betraying the tumultuous sensations he was creating in her.

She heard a deep masculine sigh and knew a small thrill in the knowledge that he was pleased with what he was seeing. Colour seeped along her cheekbones as she considered what that was. A wispy bra and string in a marriage of midnight-blue lace; legs made sexy by the natural-toned lace of hold-up stockings and by the sandals he had bought her.

Then she remembered something else. The small scar across her tummy which hadn't been there when he had seen her like this before.

Suddenly, in a ragged little plea, she was appealing to him, 'Turn off the light. Please turn off the light.'

He didn't say a word as his long firm hands spanned her midriff. Their sensuous warmth on her bare flesh made her gasp and shudder with need. Those hands were sliding down her body, over her hips and buttocks, and his tongue was finding its own path along the valley of her breasts to her waist as he dropped to his knees in front of her and pressed his lips against the fine Caesarean scar.

'You're beautiful,' he whispered.

Even with her scars? Even though she wasn't as physically perfect as he remembered her?

'So are you,' she whispered, emotion clogging her throat and her hands doing what they had been longing to do for the past few days: luxuriating in the feel of his strong black hair.

She wanted more of him. *All* of him! she thought achingly, her breath catching in her lungs as he slid back along her body to press tantalising kisses over the upper swell of each straining breast.

'Be patient. Patience...' Though he sounded breathless,

his tone was softly teasing, while his hands were playing a mercilessly tormenting game of their own.

Slipping inside the wispy-laced cups at the outer edges of her breasts, they moved beneath each aching mound to cradle its blossoming softness without actually touching the hardening and torturously sensitive peak.

When he did, forcing the lace down to free them to his fervid and appreciative gaze, Magenta strained towards him with a shuddering cry.

'That's what I liked about you,' he murmured, and even his voice was arousing her, threatening to drive her crazy along with the warm breath fanning her ear. 'You were always so immensely grateful for the smallest things.'

It was all part of his technique—this withholding of pleasure and his feigned surprise at her frenzied response when he finally gave in and granted it. She knew it—and knew she had crossed the boundaries of ecstasy with this man before. That she had let him take her where no other man had ever taken her, or ever could.

Now, guided by the map of his experience and an inherent memory of the games they'd used to play, she strained towards him, gasping as he caught her to him. And with her lips but a hair's breadth from his, she murmured, 'So fill me with undying gratitude.'

He gave a low chuckle in his throat, a sensually inspired sound, before lifting her off her feet and carrying her over to the big bed.

Her body was soft, Andreas thought appreciatively, dropping down beside her. As silky as the dress that had already slid into a blue pool beside the bed. And whatever else she had forgotten, she remembered *this,* he thought, feeling his own body responding to the way she gasped and moaned from the pleasure of his hands and lips, the way her body rose to meet the burning demands of his mouth.

He made little work of removing her bra and its matching triangle of lace, then the delicate little shoes, but when it came to removing her stockings he took an almost shameful pleasure in stringing it out.

Lying there naked, with her arms in an abandoned arc above her head, she was waiting for him to join her.

Temptation mocking him, it took every gram of his self-control not to do so immediately, not to give in to his driving urges and take them where they both wanted to go. However, it was worth the agony of waiting to watch the way her lovely eyes darkened and closed as he moved to unsheathe her beautiful legs and, with a subtle sleight of hand, just managed to skim the warm apex of her femininity as he peeled back each lacy stocking top in turn.

'Andreas...'

She was wet with desire. He could feel her moist heat against his hand.

'What is it, darling?' His own arousal was so hot and intense he could scarcely speak as she writhed against him. He needed to be naked with her, to feel every part of her lovely body beneath his.

Now, with a swift shedding of his own clothes, and taking responsibility for her protection, he came back to join her, lowering himself onto her in a meeting of pulsing flesh that made her gasp and strain urgently towards him as he groaned his satisfaction deep in his throat.

Her hands on his heated flesh were a pleasure he had never forgotten, but he revelled in the mind-blowing experience now as if it was the very first time. He wanted her like he had never wanted any woman—before or since—but he couldn't just take what he wanted like some callow youth. Whatever this woman had done to him she needed to be treated with kid gloves, and with all the consideration and care his maturity demanded.

He'd once thought he had been put on this earth solely to

pleasure Magenta James, and he did so now with all the skill of his acquired experience. Taking his time, he reacquainted himself with every secret path and byway of her body, remembering her likes, what drove her craziest, as though the last six years didn't exist. As though there hadn't been other lovers—or at least one that he knew of—who had come after him. For now he wanted to forget that—and he did.

A long time later, when she was sobbing for the one thing he was withholding, he slid his hands under her buttocks and lifted her body to accommodate his length. As soon as he started to enter her he felt her recoil almost imperceptibly, and he held himself there for a few seconds, finding her not quite as he had anticipated.

Heavens! She was tight.

Magenta gave a shuddering gasp as he moved to sink further into her softness—a sound of unbelievable pleasure after her surprising initial discomfort.

'Am I hurting you?' Andreas asked, his breathing ragged, as if he was on the brink of losing control.

She made a small murmured negation and through the waves of sensation that were washing over her wondered whether, if she had had a normal childbirth, he would even have needed to ask. But she hadn't. And it had been so long since she had done this...

Oh, but he felt so good!

As her body lifted to his he pushed more confidently inside her, deeper and deeper, until he was filling her, completing her, and then there was nothing between them and the earth-shattering pleasure of their straining flesh and their bodies locked together as one.

He started to move and she was moving with him, in a rhythm that was as natural as breathing. Each breath-catching thrust of his body was taking her with him, upwards and outwards, to scale heights of rapture such as Magenta had never conceived possible. She felt whole again for the first time since they had been together, and she clung to him as he took her to the outer edges of another universe until she was crying out from the shockwaves of pure pleasure ripping not just through her body but reaching down and opening up her mind and her soul as well.

She was his for eternity and knew she always had been, even when she had been young and foolish and fighting her attraction to him in a reckless, desperate desire to be free. As she acknowledged that fact, opening her heart to the realisation that she was and always had been hopelessly in love with him, the past rushed up on her like a tidal wave out of nowhere, bursting her defences wide open, and she saw the truth in all its shocking clarity.

At nineteen she'd believed the world was hers by right, that her face and figure were sure to get her the fame and fortune she craved. She remembered craving it to the exclusion of everything else. Her four-month affair with Andreas. His feelings for her. Even her self-respect.

She groaned inwardly as her brain reacquainted her with the selfish, mercenary creature she had been. She didn't want to remember, but the shattering experience of making love with him had severed the chains of her amnesia, and whether she was ready for it or not the last barriers of her resistance were finally caving in.

She'd been ambitious—ruthlessly so—and she hadn't planned on a man like Andreas Visconti coming into her life so soon.

'It isn't enough for me,' she had said, when he had asked her to marry him and told her about his future plans for his family's business.

But they could make a success of their lives together, he had insisted, before going on to show her just how persuasive he could be as, like always after one of their heated arguments, they both wound up in his bed.

Their rows had been tempestuous affairs, she remembered. And always over the same things. Her mother. His family. What Andreas had referred to as her 'hankering' after a career. She'd even accused him of trying to hold her back. Yet she hadn't been able to resist him, and they had both known it, but she had crushed her feelings for him by convincing herself that they were generated purely by sex and that she would probably respond in the same way to *any* attractive man she happened to fancy.

When Marcus Rushford had discovered her at the studio where she'd been getting some new photographs done for her portfolio she'd been flattered by his interest and attention. Older, worldly and debonair, with a lot of very important and influential contacts throughout the modelling profession, he had singled her out as the new face of contemporary chic—and she, like a fool, had been seduced by all his promises to make her famous.

Well, what girl wouldn't have been? she thought, striving for some justification for the way she had behaved. Living with poverty and her mother's drinking problems hadn't been easy. Neither had the stigma of those two words on her birth certificate: Father Unknown.

Just like on Theo's, she reflected, with a crushing feeling in her chest that made it almost difficult to breathe. Or at least a blank space where Andreas's name should have been. She tried reminding herself that Theo's had stayed blank for a totally different reason than hers, but that didn't help at all.

She had been taunted at school because of it, and because of her mother's reputation and the situation they had been living in. Was it any wonder she'd craved a better life? The big time? At the very least some kind of identity? she thought, harrowed.

At some point Andreas had rolled away from her and was now breathing deeply and regularly beside her. Pushing back the duvet, she slid quietly out of bed, so as not to wake him, and carried her anguishing burden of memories into the bathroom.

Finding his towelling robe hanging behind the door, she slipped it on and, huddled inside it, sank onto the luxurious mat beside the sunken Jacuzzi.

She had had her head turned by Marcus Rushford, she recalled, shamed by the memories that continued to rush back at her. Nothing else had counted but this new excitement in her life. For a girl who had had nothing, the older man's promises of having everything suddenly within her grasp had been too much to resist.

When she had been breaking up with Andreas and he had coldly challenged her to deny her feelings for him she had laughed in his face, fearful that he would use his irresistible and persuasive sexual powers to try and change her mind. 'You didn't really think I was serious about you? About *this?*' she had taunted, with regard to the restaurant and all that he had been offering. 'Did you *really* think I wanted to spend my life dishing up pizza in a cheap little café? And one I'd rather be seen dead than stuck in!'

She had been offensive and heartless. But she had been panicking inside because she had wanted to be free. Free to pursue her dreams of becoming a top model.

A few days later, guilty over how much Andreas must have spent on that special edition of Byron's poems, she'd gone to see him to return it, but done nothing to hide the evidence of another man's passion on her neck. She groaned at how sick it made her feel to remember how she had flaunted it like some prized trophy. Cruelly. Shamelessly. To the man who had wanted to marry her and whose bed she had left so recently she must have seemed contemptible. So cheap.

When she'd given him back that book he had hurled it across the room, telling her she was no good, just like her mother.

She hadn't cared. Nor had she given him any inkling that she had. Her one driving ambition had been to get on.

Selling herself to the highest bidder...

Inside the thick robe she shivered violently, fully aware of exactly what Andreas had meant. With her mother going into rehab and wanting to give up the house, Magenta had already been living in Marcus Rushford's smart, upmarket apartment.

Her big break had come only weeks after that shaming scene with Andreas, in a lucrative, high-profile contract with a hair products company. It was all she had been hoping for but she had had to turn it down, having just received the biggest shock of her life. She was pregnant—with what she knew was Andreas's child.

When Marcus had found out he had slapped her—hard. There was no way he was going to promote her, he had said, if she didn't take the necessary steps to do what she had to do.

She'd cried for a week, she remembered, reliving the anguish of that time. And at the end of it had told him there was no way that she would harm her baby. She'd taken a bus ride to the neighbourhood where she'd used to live, having decided that she would have to tell Andreas. She hadn't planned on asking him to take her back. She'd known she had behaved far too badly for that, and suspected that he probably wouldn't even believe that the child she was carrying was his, but she'd owed it to Andreas to at least give him the chance of making up his own mind.

When she had got within shouting distance of the restaurant, however, her nerve had failed her. She'd shrunk back into the doorway of a baker's shop, fear gripping her at something she'd remembered him saying.

'If you got pregnant with my baby and insisted on bringing it up alone—' as she'd threatened to do after one of their more impassioned scenarios '—then you'd better know now that I'd do all in my power to get custody of my child rather than see it brought up by a fame-crazed mother and a man-crazy, seasoned drunk of a grandmother!'

Fear such as she had never known had pressed down on her in that doorway. It was there she had realised that she wanted Andreas's baby more than she had wanted anything in her life.

She'd tried ringing him once after that, phoning the restaurant under the guise of making a booking in the hope that he would answer. Not to speak to him particularly, but simply to hear his voice. When someone else had answered she had put down the phone, too cowardly to say who she was. Later, someone whose name she couldn't even remember had told her he had gone to America.

Marcus had tried to put pressure on her when it had become clear to him that she wasn't going to give up her baby. She would blow her chances of ever becoming a model, he'd kept reminding her, pulling no punches in telling her what pregnancy would do to her figure. Either she did the sensible thing now, he'd reiterated, or she could kiss goodbye to her career *and* his apartment. It was as simple as that. Stardom or the streets.

She'd chosen the streets—or as good as. With her mother growing stronger, and renting a one-bedroom flat, Magenta had taken up her offer to let her stay on a temporary basis. Sleeping on the sofa at night, taking any job from cleaning to waitressing during the day, her only goal had been to try and save enough for a place for herself and the coming baby to live. That was until the day fate had taken a hand and she'd woken up two months later, paralysed, with a beautiful baby boy and the memory of its father and those terrible months following wiped clean from her mind.

Creeping back into the bedroom, making sure Andreas was still asleep, she gathered up her underwear and stockings and the few belongings in the bag he had bought her, and very quietly made her way back to her own room.

She had blanked it out because it had been too painful to

remember, and now it was agony coming to terms with the way she had behaved.

She recalled what Andreas had said to her in the lift that day, about her scarf hiding the marks of another man's lust, and she cringed, knowing now exactly why he had said it. But he didn't know the truth, and suddenly she was seized by the startling realisation that she couldn't tell him even now. That if she did then he'd realise that Theo was his. And she couldn't risk letting him know—not when he despised her so much. Even if it was with good reason, she accepted despairingly. That didn't alter the fact that he obviously thought she could still be bought, and that he had only made love to her now for his own satisfaction—to show her that he could. And like a fool she had fallen into his tender trap...

She was sobbing and she couldn't stop, the breath-catching pain after so much joy sending violent shudders through her entire body.

How could she have let it happen? she wondered despairingly. She'd known he despised her and now, having recalled how badly she had treated him, it wasn't any wonder that he thought her not only heartless, but promiscuous too. She had had his love and she had blown it—thrown it away as if it didn't matter. And with it whatever respect he had had for her.

Curled up in a tight ball on the bed, she thought how incredible making love with him had been. But all it had succeeded in doing was to make her fall more deeply and hopelessly in love with him. And he...

No matter how much it hurt, she thought, she had to face the truth. He had had his payback in her willing and unconditional surrender. He was too proud a man ever to allow himself to become emotionally involved with her again.

CHAPTER NINE

SHE HAD SLEPT fitfully on top of the duvet for what had remained of the night.

Rising late, she groped for her cell phone on the bedside cabinet, where she had dumped the contents of her bag, which she had then left with her dress in Andreas's bedroom. Eventually she found it in the deep pocket of the masculine robe that she was still wearing.

'Why didn't you tell me about Andreas?' she asked pointedly and without any preamble when her mother answered after the first few rings.

There was a long silence at the other end of the line.

'Why?' Magenta pressed, staring out across the grounds through one of the windows. A pheasant was wandering peacefully across the middle of the pristine lawn, its coppery plumage striking in the morning sun. 'Why didn't you tell me I'd had a relationship with him? And that my baby— my beautiful baby—was his son?'

'I thought it was for the best.' Jeanette's tone was defensive. 'I knew what that Visconti family thought of you—thought of both of us—and I wanted something better for you,' she said. 'I was relieved when you gave him up, but then afterwards, when you moved back in with me in that flat, I heard you crying every night. Sometimes when you were asleep you'd even call out his name. When you had that haemorrhage and you couldn't remember anything about him I hoped you'd forgotten him for good. I wanted you to make a fresh start. Not to have to rely on any man, or need one in your life as I always did. I didn't think it mattered if Theo didn't know who his real father was. After all, it didn't do you any harm, did it?'

No? Magenta thought with bitter self-derision, thinking of the vain and hedonistic glory-seeking creature she had been.

'You had no right to do that.' It was a small cry from the depths of her heart, stinging as it was from all she'd remembered about herself, all she had lost, and now the humiliation of winding up in bed with the man who despised her because of it.

'I was only thinking of you.' Her mother had put on her *don't be angry with me—you know I'm not strong enough to take it* voice. 'Why are you asking me all this anyway?'

'It doesn't matter now. I'll ring you later,' Magenta said wearily, unable to cope with explaining right then how she had met Andreas again, and how last night she'd remembered everything. Later, she thought, but not now. Not when she was hurting so much inside.

She was longing for a shower. She felt so groggy. And after what had happened last night between her and Andreas she didn't feel up to facing him just yet. Consequently, donning her white track top and matching joggers, and twisting her hair into a topknot, she decided that the best thing was to give herself some breathing space before she made up her mind what she was going to do.

The house appeared to be silent as she went down into the hall.

Spotting the fine gauze at the French windows through the dining room door stirring gently in the morning breeze, she decided to make a quick exit to avoid seeing anyone, and was halfway across the room when Mrs Cox's voice made her almost jump with fright.

'If you're looking for Mr Visconti he went out early,' the

housekeeper told her, from where she was arranging some bright blooms on a table behind the door. 'Would you like me to prepare your breakfast now or would you prefer to wait?'

'N-no, thanks,' Magenta stammered, her gaze on the colourful heads, utterly surprised that Andreas could just get up and go about his business as though nothing had happened. 'I mean I'll wait—thanks.' Somehow she managed a smile before slipping out onto the terrace, her lungs grasping greedily at the sweet scented air.

The morning was as refreshing as only an English morning at the height of summer could be, she thought distractedly—and, grateful for it, she instantly broke into a run.

Across the terrace, down across the lawn—she didn't ease back until she was over the little bridge that spanned the brook and well on her way through the woods.

The path was soft with leaf mould and her feet made a dull sound as they struck the ground. She thought of the first time she had done this, nearly two years after lying, paralysed, in that coma, and as she so often did, and in spite of how she was feeling, she offered up her silent thanks to everyone and everything that had pulled her through when she had thought she might never even walk again.

She wanted to keep running, but her breasts were too tender after the passion she had shared with Andreas, and with hot colour staining her cheeks at how willingly she had allowed him to use her, she slowed her pace to a brisk walk.

'Walking, Magenta?'

As though she had conjured him from her thoughts, Andreas was running up behind her. The contours of his chest and arms were emphasised by the white T-shirt he was wearing with black joggers, and with his hair slicked back he looked utterly superb.

'You're never going to stretch yourself, ambling along at this pace.' He bounced light-footedly past and turned to face her, his sparkling eyes alive with health and teasing.

'I'm stretched enough, thank you,' she responded succinctly, and then could have kicked herself for the unintended implication. She was glad when he chose to ignore it. 'I've already done my running,' she clarified. 'Besides, I'm not anatomically designed to be able to enjoy quite the same freedom as you.'

A swift glance over her anatomy beneath the zipped and clinging white top had comprehension dawning in those glinting eyes. 'Ah!' Like her, he had slowed to a walk, and was now falling into step beside her. 'Magenta, would you mind if I asked you a rather personal question?'

She sent a wary glance towards him and with a shrug said, 'Why not? You will anyway.'

His brows drew together as though he were questioning the chill in her voice. 'When did you last make love?'

His question was so unexpected that she didn't know how to respond immediately. 'You should know,' she parried, looking straight ahead.

'I'm serious, Magenta.'

He was too. A quick look at his face showed a keenly assessing absorption that she hadn't really seen in him before. But of course he had to be thinking how tight she had been last night when he had entered her—far tighter than he had probably been expecting.

'You're right.' She made a cynical little sound down her nostrils. 'It *is* a personal question.' How did you tell someone who thought the worst about you that there had only ever been one man in your life and that he was standing right in front of you? 'And all I have to say is that it shouldn't have happened.'

'Is that why you sneaked away before I was awake—and with *my* bathrobe?'

She could tell from his voice that he was trying to make light of it.

'Don't worry. You'll get it back,' she said tartly.

His hand on her arm was suddenly stopping her in her

tracks. 'The robe doesn't worry me. Your frame of mind towards me this morning does. What's wrong, Magenta?'

From the top of an ash tree near where they were standing the pure notes of a song thrush were rippling down through the dappled leaves like liquid gold.

'Are you saying you regret what happened between us?'

He was drawing her closer and Magenta's lungs seemed to lock—in contrast to Andreas's, which were still expanding deeply from where he had been running.

She wanted to speak but she couldn't, because his lips were suddenly brushing lightly across hers, sending traitorous impulses leaping along her veins.

'Don't...' she murmured tremulously, but her plea was lost beneath the shrill, lucid notes of the thrush.

'That doesn't sound like regret to me.'

There was warm satisfaction in the way he breathed against her throat, and then she felt the cool bark of a tree against her back, and his fingers dealing with the zipper of her top.

His hands were like some craved addiction, making her cry out with the satisfaction that they alone could supply.

As he took her mouth with his she moved involuntarily against him, stimulated by the warm contoured muscles straining beneath his T-shirt, aware of his arousal that was every bit as strong as hers through the light, silky material of his joggers.

When he cupped her aching femininity she could have let herself go and taken the release she was craving right there and then. But the shrieking of a blackbird as it flew up from somewhere close by in agitated alarm brought her to her senses.

'No—don't!'

In an instant she was pulling away from him, breathing deeply to restore the sanity she could so easily have lost as her trembling fingers struggled to reinstate her top.

'Magenta…' He sounded breathless, and his strong features revealed just how much he was fighting for control.

'No!' she said adamantly, to herself more than to Andreas, and she started to run from him, not stopping until she came back across the little bridge, wondering how she was ever going to say what she had to say when he only had to touch her to blow all her firm decisions to smithereens.

He was right beside her as she came across the lawn towards the back of the house and saw a beautiful bronze Mini parked there on the shingle by the terrace steps.

'You've got a visitor,' she observed, dismayed. All she had been hoping to do was take a shower and then somehow find the courage to tell Andreas that she couldn't possibly stay there in his home another minute. How could she ever reclaim her self-respect if she did?

'No,' he said unequivocally, pulling a key out of the pocket of his joggers. 'Take it. It's yours,' he informed her, handing it to her.

Magenta's immediate instinct was to recoil from his offer 'What's this for?' she challenged. 'Services rendered?' She couldn't believe how much she was hurting inside.

He shot her a surprisingly censuring look. 'For services yet to be fulfilled,' he enlightened her. 'If you're going to be working for me—however long it's going to be—you're going to need some form of transport. I can't always put a car and Simon at your disposal.'

'Andreas.' She had stopped on the verge of the lawn where it met the shingle drive, refusing to take the key he was still holding out to her. 'I really don't think this is a good idea. Us working together.'

'Working together?' He was looking at her askance, his sapphire eyes too intense, too probing. 'Or do you mean sleeping together?'

'Yes. No. I mean both.'

A thick eyebrow lifted almost indiscernibly. 'You didn't seem to have too many qualms about it last night.'

'Last night I was…affected.'

'By what?' he challenged roughly. 'It certainly wasn't alcohol. You didn't even sip that champagne you were given for the toasts.'

'You know what I mean. Last night changes everything.'

'Why? Because you refuse to admit that there's something between us that even you can't fight?'

'It's only sex.' *Dear heaven! Listen to me!* she thought, despairing at herself, and wondered at the dark emotion that flitted across his face.

'Yes, I know,' he accepted phlegmatically. 'But we always knew that, didn't we? Or at least *you* did. Is it so bad, meeting me on the same level now? Surely it's preferable to come together on equal terms, knowing there's no commitment or strings attached on either side. Knowing that I'm not going to embarrass you by dropping to my knees and asking you to marry me this time. Knowing that no one's going to get hurt.'

Only me, Magenta thought. Because now Andreas Visconti had learned his lesson. There was no way he would ever open his heart or lay his emotions on the line for her again.

'I'm not staying here,' she told him firmly. 'And I'm not taking the car. Oh, I know you think I can be bought. And, all right, maybe I let myself be bought once. But like you I learnt the hard way that what we want isn't always right for us, and that all the things we think are important can be wiped out in just a minute. As for material things—well, they just don't count. So I'd rather not be made to feel indebted to you, if it's all the same to you.'

Her hands were stuffed inside the front-facing pockets of her track top as she started walking again, her eyes focussing straight ahead on the house while she strove to blink bright, betraying tears away, her trainers crunching over the shingle.

'Is that why you left the dress in my room? And the other

things I bought you? Because they made you feel indebted to me?'

'What do you think?' She didn't even look at him, just kept on walking.

'I told you they were a business expense,' he reminded her.

'Well, that's a fancy name for it, isn't it?' she decried bitterly. 'You wanted me in your bed just to satisfy a warped need for revenge. I knew it and I still went ahead and slept with you. But I've remembered, Andreas. I remember everything. I just hadn't realised until now how much you must have wanted to hurt me. And OK, perhaps it was with good cause—but can you have any idea of how I'm feeling now?'

'Magenta—'

'Yes, I'll bet you can!' She carried on across the drive, past the beautiful bronze car that would have made the young Magenta jump at the chance of owning it. She sent only a disparaging glance towards it. 'Well, you've paid me back, and you must be feeling *so* good—especially in view of the amazingly short time you had to wait! But I'm not going to—'

'Magenta!' Hard fingers caught her arm as she mounted the terrace steps, pulling her to a swift and determined stop. 'What happened...happened. There wasn't any intended sense of revenge or malice behind it.'

He'd moved just one step higher than she was, but appeared to tower disconcertingly above her.

'Ha!' She tried to move past him and found her efforts blocked by his superb masculine body. 'Let me pass.'

'No. Not until I've said what I have to say.'

She looked up into the hard severity of his tightly controlled features, her expression pained and wounded in the sunlight.

'I'll admit it started out that way, with me wanting to give you a taste of your own medicine. But revenge is a pretty cold bedfellow, and I don't want to dwell on the past any more than you do. I made love to you last night because there wasn't anything in the world I wanted to do more. And if you remember I let *you* make the decision. I didn't force your hand.'

'But you knew that if you kissed me I wouldn't have any choice in the matter.'

'No, I didn't know that. I thought because of what you'd said when things got rather heated down there that evening in the garden you'd just tell me to go to hell.'

'I wish I had!'

'Why? Because then you'd still be hiding behind the safety of your lost memory? Is that how you would have preferred it?'

Guilt and shame propelled her forward, but as she tried to make her escape again his arms came up to stop her. His chest felt solid beneath her hands, making her gasp with the betraying sensations that even now were mocking her decision to leave.

'Let's just accept that last night satisfied something in both of us—whatever it was that needed to be satisfied. But I'm not having you cutting off your nose to spite your face just because you're nursing a very strong case of hurt pride. You need this job, and I sure as hell don't want all the hassle of trying to find another temporary assistant when you've adapted to the position far more easily and effectively than someone who had been doing it for years.

'I don't want to be the result of you and your little boy winding up homeless—or dependent upon your great-aunt, if that's how you'd both end up. As for the car... Whatever feelings I might have been harbouring about you, life dealt you a pretty miserable hand all round—especially after we broke up. I was only trying to make things a little easier for you. It wasn't meant as a trinket with which to buy your favours or more delightful interludes like last night.

'And don't pretend it wasn't delightful,' he chided softly, when she turned her head, her jaw clenching against the responses his words were producing in her. 'For both of us.

Whatever you feel about it now. Go home, by all means,' he
acceded, 'but take the car. It's a company vehicle. I had Simon
take me up to the office to pick it up for you this morning,' he
enlightened her—which at least went some way to explaining
why he'd left without waking her or even leaving a message
for her earlier. 'You can use it until... Well, until this assignment ends...or until you cease to work for my company—
whichever is the longer.'

He had obviously made up his mind that she'd be in the
office on Monday morning.

'It isn't—' It isn't going to work, she was about to say. But
the shrill ring of his cell phone cut her dead.

'Magenta!'

She heard his urgent command but she was already running up the steps, away from him. She was relieved when,
catching the sudden impatience with which she heard him
speaking, she realised that he had stopped pursuing her to
take the call instead.

She couldn't take the car because it would symbolise just
another payment from him, she thought bitterly when she
stepped under the jets of the shower a few minutes later.
Like the dress and its accoutrements. Like this job. Which
was why she couldn't possibly carry on working for him for
another day. If she agreed to do so then she would be letting
him manipulate her, as he had been doing from the beginning, she thought wretchedly. But that didn't stop her mourn-
ing the young man who had worshipped her, read her poetry
and given her gifts he could scarcely afford, who had argued
for her against his family's harsh judgement. In contrast to
the mature Andreas, who could afford to give her everything
now. Everything, that was, except his love...

A knock on her bedroom door as she was towelling herself dry had her quickly shrugging into a white cotton robe.
Her stomach turned over when she saw Andreas standing
there outside her door.

'I have to fly to Paris for an urgent meeting and I won't be back until late tomorrow evening,' he told her, sounding none too pleased about the prospect.

He'd obviously already showered, because his hair was curling damply against the clean white shirt he'd put on under his dark suit, and it was difficult to ignore what his cologne was doing to her. He was, Magenta thought achingly, with sensual shivers running through her, the epitome of every woman's fantasy.

'You can stay here if you wish, or if you prefer, and you're still being obstinate about taking the car, I'll get Simon to drive you home.'

She nodded, because if she argued she was afraid he'd try and talk her out of what she knew she had to do.

'If that's the case, then I'll see you in the office on Monday morning.'

She didn't answer this time, and when he tilted her chin to kiss her gently on the mouth she had to clench her hands at her sides to stop herself from throwing her arms around his neck and pulling him down to her.

Goodbye, Andreas.

Five minutes later she saw the Mercedes haring out of the drive as if the hounds of hell were after it. An hour later she was riding home in a cab, out of his life.

CHAPTER TEN

THE LITTLE BAY pony was being put through its paces, and from the wooden fence enclosing the beginners' arena Magenta waved to the little figure in riding hat and jodhpurs sitting astride the animal's back.

She had thought Theo might want her to accompany him, as this was his first time on a horse, but he had been happy to leave her standing on the sidelines and had gone off with only the riding instructor instead.

Independent. Like Andreas, she thought, praying the day would be a long time coming when his son wouldn't need her as she watched the boy and the pony walking away from her now, guided by the young woman out into the wider field.

She hadn't heard from Andreas since she had left his house two weeks ago, leaving her formal typed notice on his desk, terminating a contract she hadn't even signed.

He hadn't bothered to contact her. But then what reason would he have? she asked herself torturously. He had had his revenge when she had fallen into bed with him, just as he had predicted she would. The only contact she had had from him or his firm since had been in the form of a cheque that he had had paid into her bank account, representing what she could only calculate had to be three months' salary.

Not wanting to take anything from him other than that which was her due, she had almost sent back the unearned income—until a trip to sign on at the local Job Centre had again brought her to her senses. If he hadn't prevented her from taking the job she had actually applied for she wouldn't now be desperately trying to find another. And if compensating her for that was his way of easing his conscience, then it was a small price to pay on his part for having his revenge—and at her expense!

She waved to Theo again through a blur of tears as he completed his first few metres of a rising trot. He was preoccupied, though, and didn't look her way. Already leaving her, she thought with an absurd ache in her chest.

Her brain only half registered a car drawing to a halt in the stableyard just behind her. From one of the open stalls, another horse whinnied softly. Another child being brought to its lesson, she thought absently. The stables were probably very popular on Saturday mornings.

She was just wondering with crushing anguish how she was going to explain to Theo that this first of the riding lessons he had longed for was, for a while at least, going to have to be his last, when she felt a prickling sensation travel down her spine.

'Hello, Magenta.'

For a few beats her heart seemed to stand still, and then she was swinging round, her loose hair falling over the powder-blue T-shirt she wore with jeans and pumps like dark rippling silk.

'Wh-what are you doing here?' She knew her stammering had nothing to do with any problem with her speech and everything to do with the shock of seeing Andreas there.

'Looking for you.'

As usual he was dressed for business, and as usual he looked cool and calm and collected. Probably going to some important meeting—or just back from one, she decided with a stray glance at the Mercedes. The dark executive image of the man looming above her was doing chaotic things to her already strained and now tingling nerves.

'How did you find me?'

His mouth compressed, and against the backdrop of the rustic stableyard he cut an incongruous yet striking figure with his elegant designer clothes and his dark hair ruffled slightly by the cooling wind.

'Purely by chance. I called at your home first, and your neighbour from the flat above was just coming out. She said you'd told her you were bringing Theo for his first riding lesson today and suggested I try here first.'

Her fifty-something neighbour probably would have relished doing that, Magenta thought, deciding that it probably wasn't 'purely by chance' that the woman had come down just as Andreas was knocking at her door. Even here the luxurious car and its affluent owner were attracting the attention of two stable girls as they passed, one carrying a saddle, the other a bucket, before disappearing into one of the open stalls.

'Why?' Magenta enquired poignantly, looking up into his strong dark features.

'Because of the way you left. Without a word or any prior warning. Without even talking it over with me personally first.'

'I left my formal resignation. I didn't feel that any further explanations were necessary.'

She heard him take a breath before he came and rested his hand, like her, on the top bar of the fence, his body half turned towards her. He was so close that she could feel the pull of his dark chemistry evoking dangerous sensations in her, making her pulse quicken, her body yearn to lean closer to him.

'Is this Theo?' A jerk of his chin indicated the trotting pony and its little rider.

'Yes.' She couldn't even look at Andreas as she said it.

'He looks like he's been born to it.'

Magenta uttered a tight little laugh, clinging to the fence

with both hands now as if it was the only thing holding her upright. She remembered going riding sometimes with Andreas in the distant past, how she hadn't really taken to it, while *he* had ridden as proudly and confidently as his ancient forebears.

'Like you were born to drive men mad, Magenta.'

He had turned towards the field and was following the little boy's progress with studied absorption—as if he hadn't just landed a comment that had set her veins on fire.

'Then that's their misfortune,' she said swiftly, unable to keep the bitterness out of her voice. All her life, because of the way she looked, she had had more than her fair share of masculine attention.

'Yes.'

She didn't even need to ask to realise he was referring to himself. For a few moments they stood in silence, both gazing ahead at the pony, which was walking now, being led around in a figure of eight.

'I want you to come back,' Andreas said at length.

Magenta sent him a sidelong glance. 'As your PA?' When he didn't answer, she thought, *Of course. What else?* She'd probably caused him quite a bit of inconvenience, walking out as she had. 'Why?' Her eyes were wounded, wary. 'To save you all the bother of having to find someone else? I thought you would have replaced me—' she clicked her thumb and middle finger together '—just like that.'

The strong jaw tightened, as though he was restraining an element of impatience. 'I know you won't let me help in any way, no matter how much you might need it, but I'd like you at least to have the benefit of earning the salary you expected to be earning after I prevented you from getting the job you'd set your heart on.'

'Why? Because your conscience is probing you now and you suddenly feel responsible for me? I don't want your pity,' she breathed, with an excruciating ache deep in her chest.

'That's good,' he returned. 'Because I wasn't offering any. But as your employer…well, let's just say I acted more than a little unethically.'

'Unethically?' She gave a dry, brittle little laugh. 'And as my ex-lover?'

He didn't answer. After all, what could he say?

She saw him rest his elbows on the fence, his hands—those hands that had the power to do what no other man could ever do to her—clasped absently together in front of him.

'I convinced myself you owed me something, Magenta,' he admitted surprisingly, 'and as a consequence of that I find myself owing you.'

'If that's meant as an apology,' she uttered, 'forget it. I have.' That couldn't have been further from the truth. But her pride would never let her admit to him how much her folly in imagining she could work for him—for whatever reason she had convinced herself she needed to—had cost her emotionally. Far, far more even than financially.

'I'm afraid that doesn't fall within my rules of conduct as a human being. You said you found it difficult getting a good job because of the discrimination you encountered when you told prospective employers what had happened to you, and I robbed you of a chance without even knowing about it, or what you had been through. But if you hadn't had that setback which sent Rushford packing—I'm assuming that's what happened—then without a shadow of a doubt, with your single-minded ambition and determination, you would have been enjoying all the status and financial rewards of a top model now.'

Sucking in her breath, Magenta stared at the pony that was now trotting again with its animated little rider. Theo had only just spotted the tall man who was talking to her and he kept looking towards Andreas, completely distracted from whatever it was the instructor was saying to him.

Since her little boy had come home Magenta hadn't been

able to get over how much he looked like Andreas, and it struck her again forcefully now. The resemblance, though, had done nothing to jog her memory of Andreas *before* she'd met him again in that wine bar, and a little shudder ran through her at recalling the conversation she had had with her great-aunt when she had brought Theo home to Magenta last week.

'Have you told him?'

It had been one of the first things the woman had asked her as soon as she had stepped through the door, and Magenta hadn't even needed to ask who she meant.

'No, I haven't,' she'd admitted after she'd released Theo from her heart-swelling hug and he'd scampered off to play the DVD that Aunt Josie's stepdaughter had given him. With that she had broken down in those plump maternal arms and poured out the whole miserable story.

'I still think you'd better tell him, young lady,' the woman had advocated as they'd followed Theo into Magenta's clean and tidy yet shabby-looking sitting room. 'From what you've said about him he doesn't sound to me like a man who'd appreciate being deceived.'

Now, hurting and angry at the way he was continuing to judge her, and for allowing herself to be so deeply and hopelessly in love with him, she flung caution to the winds and tossed back a response to his remark about her single-minded determination. 'Well, that's where you're wrong. For a start Marcus Rushford was off the scene long before you're suggesting. And it *wasn't* my brain haemorrhage that put paid to my glorious career as a model. It was over long before that because I wouldn't give up *your* son!'

She wasn't even looking at him. Nevertheless she could feel his shock as tangibly as the cool wind that was penetrating her thin T-shirt.

'What are you saying?'

His sentence was little more than a rasped whisper. Perplexity clouded the eyes raking over her face, looking for some sign of clarification before they shifted to Theo, to Magenta, than back to the little boy again.

'Are you telling me he's *mine?*' His features as he turned back to her were contorted with disbelief.

'Look at him, Andreas, if you don't believe me.'

His doubting gaze returned to the child, and this time he couldn't take his eyes off him. His strong face was criss-crossed by a myriad of emotions. Bewilderment. Incredulity. And something else. Something that was beginning to look remarkably like acceptance.

'I don't understand. You were using protection.'

She shrugged. 'It happens.'

'And you were with Rushford...'

'Not in that way.'

Deep lines scored his face as he turned interrogating eyes in her direction. 'What are you saying?'

'I'm saying that—'

'Mummy—look!'

She broke off to see the pony being led back towards the stableyard. Theo was sitting proudly in the saddle, his arms outstretched on either side of him, the reins hanging loosely over the pony's back.

'Darling, be careful!' she called out.

At the same time Andreas was punching a number into his cell phone.

Of course. He probably had somewhere important to be, Magenta thought, realising with a stab of despair that he could only be attending to business at a time like this if he didn't believe her.

'Yes. Cancel my meeting,' he instructed abruptly. There was a wealth of determination in the eyes that clashed with hers.

The gentle clip-clop of hooves on tarmac, however, signified that Theo's lesson was over. Gratefully Magenta tore herself away from Andreas, glad of these few minutes when she could occupy herself with getting her son out of the saddle and so delay the moment when the ultimate interrogation came.

'Who's that, Mummy?' As the instructor handed her the pony's reins in order to go and attend to something in its stable Theo pointed towards Andreas who, to Magenta's dismay, had followed her across the yard. From his vantage point in the saddle, Theo was studying him seriously, his head tilted to one side. 'Are you Mummy's friend?'

Two pairs of identical blue eyes met and locked. 'Do you want me to be Mummy's friend?' Andreas asked.

The odd inflexion in his voice caused something inside Magenta to twist.

'Yeah! Yeah! *Yeah!*' Theo clapped his hands, so excited that it made the pony start.

Immediately Andreas's hand came up, at the same time as Magenta's, to steady the animal's head. Magenta quickly withdrew hers, feeling the havoc of his accidental touch like a collision of stars.

'Does that mean we can ride in your great big car?'

'Theo...' Magenta cautioned. Getting into Andreas's car was the last thing she wanted to do.

'You bet it does!' Andreas promised. While the child was looking excitedly towards the Mercedes he said to Magenta, 'May I?'

She nodded in response to his gesture to lift Theo off the pony, and yet he still enquired of his son, 'Would you like a hoist out of that saddle, little man?'

'Yeah! Yeah! *Yeah!*' Theo exclaimed again.

Watching the gentle way in which Andreas lifted their son down from the pony, and seeing the two of them together at last, Magenta felt as though her heart was being squeezed.

'It suits you,' she whispered, racked by emotion, but earned herself only a ravaged look from him before he set Theo safely down on his feet.

The stable girl had come back and was taking the reins from Magenta.

'You're both coming home with me,' Andreas told her as the girl led the pony back to its stall.

'I can't. Aunt Josie's cooking lunch for us,' she said, grabbing Theo by the hand as another, larger horse was being led into the yard.

It sounded a lame excuse after he had just cancelled what was doubtless an important meeting, having found out he was a father. She knew, though, that he would demand to know why she hadn't told him he had a son, and she didn't feel like explaining—especially when the fear that had kept her silent when she'd first found out she was pregnant, and again more recently, was still as rampant in her as it had ever been.

'What's wrong, Magenta? Afraid to be alone with me?' he suggested with an edge of steel in his voice, yet softly enough so that Theo couldn't hear.

Well, she was, wasn't she? she thought with a little shiver, but she said only, 'Of course not.'

'Then perhaps dear Aunt Josie won't mind stretching lunch four ways,' he proposed, the endearment mocked by his cynical tone. 'After all, I think it's time I met this paragon of virtue who had leave to look after my child when I wasn't even allowed to know I had one.'

'You were in America!' Magenta exhaled, knowing it was yet another black mark against her in his long list of grievances.

His jaw was set rigid as they came up to the car. 'Not two weeks ago!'

It didn't help Magenta telling herself that she deserved his anger as he held the car door open for the little boy to scramble onto the back seat.

'You've had him to yourself for five years,' he rasped as she stepped into the car beside her son. 'And if he really is mine then things are going to change. As of now!'

* * *

Josie Ashton was wearing her apron with a cheery fireside scene when she opened the front door of her modest home. A labourer's cottage, with just two rooms up and two down, and the addition of a small bathroom on the back, it was one of a terrace of twelve homes fronting onto a street that had been built for the workforce of a nineteenth-century printing factory, which had since been pulled down to accommodate a more lucrative and modern trading estate at the end of the road.

'Aunt Josie, this is Andreas Visconti,' Magenta told her uncomfortably, conscious that Theo was still standing there looking up at him with a kind of hero-worship instead of rushing in and down the passage as he usually did.

'Well, I didn't think he was the window-cleaner,' Josie expressed, with a grimace at the gleaming Mercedes that looked even more out of place parked outside her humble home than it had outside Magenta's flat a couple of streets away.

'Andreas, this is my great-aunt. Josie Ashton.'

'I'm pleased to meet you, Mrs Ashton,' Andreas said, shaking her hand and taking her a little off-guard, Magenta realised, with his effortless charm.

'And I suppose you're hungry too.'

Josie Ashton never did stand on ceremony, Magenta thought, but from the glow that lit the woman's face as she held the door open for them all Magenta could tell that her aunt had warmed instantly to Andreas Visconti.

The smell of roast chicken and parsnips met them as they stepped inside.

'That's very kind of you, Mrs Ashton, and I do regret having to turn down your offer, but I have some pressing business to discuss with Magenta. I hope it won't inconvenience you too much if I take her away for an hour or so?'

'Not at all,' Josie Ashton responded with obvious and increasing pleasure, unaware of the tension that was twisting

Magenta's stomach muscles into tight knots. 'Take all the time you need, Andreas. It won't be any trouble reheating her lunch.'

'I'll only be a little while,' she told Theo, stroking his dark hair.

As she stooped to kiss him, however, he scampered back along the passage towards Andreas, saying, 'I want to come too. I want to ride in Mr 'Conti's big car.'

'Not now, darling. You have to stay here and eat all the lovely lunch that Aunt Josie's cooked you,' Magenta explained gently, trying to pacify him.

But the little boy, usually so well-behaved, was having none of it.

'Why can't I come? I want another ride in Mr 'Conti's car.' He was practically in tears now.

'Hey! What's all this?' Andreas asked softly, dropping to his haunches so that his eyes were on the same level as the little boy's.

'I want to come with you,' Theo sobbed, and then, to everyone's amazement, he wound his arms tightly around Andreas's neck.

Magenta darted an anxious glance towards her aunt—who didn't notice, or was choosing not to.

'I'm flattered, Theo.' There was no mistaking the surprised emotion in the deep, masculine voice. 'But if just this time you'll stay here and look after your aunt, I'll be back for you later, I promise.'

Alarm bells started clanging ominously inside Magenta's head even as Andreas's statement went some way to pacifying the little boy.

'You shouldn't have said that,' she rebuked as soon as he had stepped into the car beside her. 'You should never make promises you can't keep.'

'Don't tell me what I should or shouldn't say, Magenta,' he warned, fastening his seat belt across his body with swift, economical movements. 'And, believe me, I *never* break promises. I'd appreciate it if you didn't say anything at all to me for a while,' he said as he pulled away, 'Because the way I feel towards you right at this moment, my dearest, I'm angry enough to bloody well crash this car!'

Andreas was sitting grim-mouthed as he steered the Mercedes through the heavy midday traffic, bringing it up onto the ring road and out of the hubbub of the crowded city.

When he had come back from Paris two weeks ago to find Magenta gone from the house he'd automatically assumed that she would turn up at the office the following day—until he had found the note she had left on his desk in the study.

He shouldn't have been surprised that she had walked out on him, but he had—and shockingly so. Especially as she hadn't said anything about leaving after their conversation in the woods or before he'd driven off for that meeting the previous day.

He had told himself it was for the best. That there was no way he would ever lay himself open to her fickle charms again. That he had suffered enough the first time. But there was something about this woman that he had never been able to prevent getting under his skin.

Even while he'd been telling himself that it was safer for his sanity's sake that she had gone from his life and—even more importantly—from his bed, some masochistic part of him had needed to see her again. A need to redress the wrong in the hardship he must have caused her had been a convenient excuse to delude himself over his main reason for wanting to see her. Because he darn well couldn't help himself! he realised, with tension gripping the hard sweep of his jaw. And all the time she had been able to simply walk away from him without even telling him he had a son!

As he followed the signs and took the slip road to a local beauty spot he realised that, despite all the possibilities that might have had him questioning her claim to paternity, there was no doubt in his mind at all that little Theo James was his. The boy had his colouring, his eyes and he looked just like he did in a photograph he had of himself playing cricket with his father at the same age. But why had Magenta denied him the right even to see his own son? Taken it on herself to keep his identity hidden?

Well, she had some explaining to do, he promised himself as he brought the car off the slip road to the roundabout. And she was going to have to make it good!

Magenta looked at him guardedly as he stopped the car in a deserted lay-by. They were high on a hill, among acres of grassland and managed forestry, and way down, through a bank of trees, she could see the glinting blue water of a reservoir or some sort of man-made lake.

'Why didn't you tell me?' he rasped. He was looking intently ahead, out of the windscreen, as though seeing something other than the white line along the quiet road. 'Why did you let me think he was Rushford's son?'

'I didn't. That was something you decided for yourself from the beginning.'

'But you didn't put me straight, Magenta. Why?'

She looked away, catching a glimpse through the trees of a white sail down there on the wind-ruffled lake. 'I don't know. I was afraid.'

'Of what?'

'Of losing him.'

'Losing him?' His tone was harsh and penetrating.

'To you and your family.'

'So you preferred to see him deprived of a father instead? Leading the disadvantaged existence he's leading now?'

'He isn't *disadvantaged!*' It was a ringing little cry, torn out of her guilt and anguish at being made to feel that she was somehow less than an adequate mother.

'Or were you intending that Marcus Rushford—or even some other man—would somehow be able to take my place and fill the breach?'

'No. I told you. Marcus was never anything other than my managing agent.'

'And you *really* expect me to believe that?'

'I don't care what you believe,' she tossed back, opening her door. 'It's the truth.'

She felt the tugging wind through her thin top as she jumped out, slamming the car door behind her. She heard him get out and close his door with far more respect than she had shown hers.

'Anyway, I did try to tell you,' she said defensively, stepping onto a grassy bank which sloped gently downhill before levelling off some distance away, offering a far better view over the lake.

'When?' Andreas pressed, following her.

'Not long after I found out I was pregnant. I knew you had the right to know.'

'That was very generous of you.' His sarcasm was flaying. 'So what changed your mind?'

'You did.'

'I did?' He gave a snort of disbelief as he drew level with her.

'I came all the way to the restaurant one day,' she explained, keeping her eyes trained on the little sailboat whose skipper was finding it hard to keep a straight course in the buffeting wind. 'But then I lost my nerve because I remembered what you'd said about if ever I got pregnant and wouldn't marry you. You said you'd fight me for custody. And that was how possessive you were simply over a hypothetical child!'

Crossing her arms, she moved down to a levelled-off viewing point.

Aware of him right behind her, she murmured, 'I was also worried that you might not believe that he was yours.'

She could almost see the derision lifting his eyebrow before he said, 'Whatever gave you *that* idea?' But she chose not to respond to his censuring remark.

While he was still so angry, and so obviously hardened towards her, she couldn't tell him the whole truth and put her heart on the line.

'I tried to ring you once, but you weren't there. Shortly afterwards I bumped into a girl we both knew one day when I was out shopping and she told me you'd gone to America. After I'd had the haemorrhage,' she added resignedly, 'I couldn't have let you know even if you'd been around—because I didn't even remember who you were.'

'Surely you must have told someone you knew—or at least your mother—who the father of your child was?' His tone was no less sceptical as he moved to stand beside her.

'Yes.'

'So what did you think whenever my name was mentioned? Didn't it even arouse your curiosity enough for you to try and find out who and where I was? Didn't you even care enough to want to find out?'

'I would have—if she'd mentioned you to me,' Magenta admitted, wondering how she could possibly explain her mother's silence without discrediting her character too much in his eyes. 'But she didn't. I think she thought there had been something going on between us that would upset me too much if I remembered it and she just wanted me to get well.'

He made a sound of angry disbelief, and she couldn't blame him. She couldn't forget how stunned and angry she had been herself when she had found out.

'So what did she tell you? That Rushford was the father? Or did she imagine you'd think your child had been produced out of thin air?'

'Andreas, don't...' It was bad enough that he was angry

with *her* without his turning his understandable venom on her mother. 'She didn't know what to tell me,' she uttered in the woman's defence, though she was still hurting unbearably because of it, and could see no reason for the way her mother had acted.

'I see.' From the grim cast of his mouth and the way his breath shivered through his nostrils he had clearly grasped the full extent of the situation. 'So she willingly put her grandson in the same situation as she put her daughter. With no father. No security. No—'

'Stop it!' She couldn't go on listening to him slating her mother, no matter how much he believed the woman deserved it, but above everything else she couldn't stand his pain.

'And what about *you*, Magenta?' he asked. 'Or is it an inherited trait of the James women to keep their children's fathers in the dark about their paternity?'

'No!'

'Then why didn't you tell me two weeks ago? Three?' His eyes scoured hers as he pulled her to face him. 'Just when was it exactly that you remembered who I am?'

The torment in his face was palpable, shredding her heart into what felt like a thousand pieces. 'That first night in the wine bar,' she admitted guiltily. 'It was an instinctive feeling rather than anything real, but over the next few hours—days—things started coming back.'

'And you didn't *tell* me?' Hard incredulity burned in his eyes as he let her go. 'All the time we were together at the house? Not even that night we made love?'

'I told you—I was afraid. You're rich now, and I don't have two cents to rub together.'

'What's that got to do with anything?' he demanded impatiently.

'I didn't want you using your money and your newfound power to hurt me. I was frightened sick you'd try and take him away from me.'

'And you didn't think it was any less of a crime trying to keep his existence from *me?*'

She did, but she didn't know what else to say to try and exonerate herself, when really there was no excuse for what she had done.

'At first I was just afraid,' she told him. 'But I didn't know what I was frightened of. There was this threat hanging over me—over Theo—and I knew it had to be because of something you'd once said or done. You already seemed to disapprove of him being left with Aunt Josie and you didn't even know he was yours! Anyway, things kept coming back in dribs and drabs. Then that night we made love I remembered everything. Until then a lot of pieces of my memory were still missing and my mind was a jumbled mess.'

'If you *have* remembered everything,' he said.

'What do you mean?' she queried, the face upturned to his etched with anxious lines.

A cold gust blew up from the lake, sweeping through the trees and penetrating her T-shirt. She wrapped her arms around herself to try and stop her shivering.

Without a word Andreas was removing his jacket.

'What do you mean?' she asked again, tortured by his sudden nearness, by his warmth and the fragrance of his cologne that was clinging to the jacket he was now placing carefully around her shoulders.

'I mean that you're still stating that Marcus Rushford wasn't your lover. Unless it's only me you're trying to convince, but your insistence does make me wonder.'

'I do remember. *Everything.* And he wasn't,' she reiterated adamantly.

'It was him you left me for. Him you wanted to be with,' he reminded her—as though she needed reminding.

'I thought I did,' she admitted. 'But it didn't take much more than a week for me to realise I didn't. OK, he was exciting, and he was offering so much, and I was young and naive enough to believe that any man could make me feel the way you did. That what we had wasn't important and I could just walk away. I didn't want to be stifled by commitment, to relinquish all my hopes and dreams. You were expecting too much and I wasn't ready, even though I really, really didn't want to break up with you.'

Emotion was threatening to overwhelm her.

'I couldn't stay at the bottom of the pile with—as you said just now—no security and no prospects, no clue as to where I'd even come from,' she said, managing to contain the sob that just for a moment had started to make her voice wobble. 'The girl with no father and most of the time no mother. With no money and no respect from anyone. Always the one who people pointed a finger at. The one who didn't quite measure up. I was determined to break free from all that, and when Marcus offered me the chance I jumped up and grabbed it.

'I truly believed he'd make me rich and famous and everyone would look at me and say, "Hasn't she done well? Jeanette James's bastard daughter. Who would have thought it, with her background and the type of upbringing she had?" I wanted respect and admiration, but above all else I wanted acceptance. To be able to show everyone who'd doubted me or shunned me—like your father and your grandmother, and all the kids I'd gone to school with—that I was every bit as good as they were. Yes, I wanted fame, and I wanted self-sufficiency. And somewhere among all those crazy mixed-up ideas of grandeur I wanted to help Mum.'

'So you didn't love him?' It was a cool, emotionless question. 'Is that what you're saying?'

'Yes.'

'Yet you still went ahead and slept with him? Moved in with him?'

Suddenly Andreas's voice seemed to be thickened by something. What was it? Magenta wondered. Disgust?

'No!' she denied fiercely, determined to put him straight.

'He offered me the use of his apartment because he'd just bought another one nearer his company and he didn't want to let it out. He wanted someone to look after it for him for a while. He said it would be better for my image to be living there rather than in "the hovel", as he called it, I'd been living in with Mum. He *wanted* us to be lovers, but I wasn't ready for that. I'm not saying we didn't kiss, because I did have a mild flirtation with him, and he did everything in his power to try and get me into bed. But it didn't take him long to guess that I still hadn't got you out of my system.

'When he knew I was coming to see you that day with that book I think he realised that you'd only have to touch me to send all his plans for my future awry. He said he'd only promote me if you were well and truly out of my life. That's when he... Well, you remember that...bruise...for want of a better word...on my neck? It was a deliberate act of brutality to stamp his mark on me before I saw you, even though he didn't stand a cat in hell's chance of getting me into bed. I think what mattered to him most was losing a marketable commodity—which was all I really was to him. He already had a long-suffering woman-friend in tow. But I was living in his flat for just a fraction of the rent, and he was already negotiating a big contract for me. I didn't want to give it all up and go back to my old life and the situation I'd been living in, so I did exactly as he told me to do that day. I knew that if you thought he had become my lover you'd never want to see me again, and I wanted to make you hate me so that you wouldn't try.'

'Why are you telling me this now?' His voice sounded almost hoarse. 'Because you're worried that I might take Theo away from you?'

Because I love you!

His face was such a hard, inscrutable mask that she couldn't say it. If she did then he could go away, satisfied that he had the ultimate triumph: Magenta James as crazy over him as he had been over her six years ago. And even if she deserved it, she couldn't take the humiliation of that.

'I don't want you to go on thinking the worst about me,' she answered steadily at length, but it was an effort when she was trembling so much inside. 'I know what I did wasn't very nice, but I just wanted you to know that I'm not entirely as bad as you would have me painted.'

'So what happened when the wonderful Marcus found out you were pregnant and had ruined all his plans?' he asked scathingly.

Flinching still from the resurrected memory, Magenta refrained from telling Andreas about the other man's brutal response. 'I was asked to leave the apartment when it become clear to him that I wasn't going to do "the sensible thing",' she informed him with bitter cynicism. 'I was planning to leave anyway. He just accelerated my departure, that's all.'

'And you went where?'

'To the new flat the council had given Mum when she left rehab.'

His features hardened but he didn't say anything.

'Then, three weeks before Theo was due… Well, you know the rest. I woke up from my coma thinking I'd lost him, but he was alive and well and almost two months old to the day. When they brought him in to see me I didn't have any strength in my arms to hold him. I was frightened that I was never going to be able to. He became my reason to recover. To get well.'

'And I wasn't there.'

Those four simple words conveyed an intensity of emotion before he looked away towards the lake, though Magenta knew he wasn't actually seeing a thing. His teeth were gritted and his face appeared slashed by some inner conflict.

'My son was brought into this world with his mother unconscious and a father who didn't even know of his existence!'

His self-condemnation was paramount, but Magenta could sense a multitude of other emotions in him too.

'Don't be too angry with me, Andreas,' she begged, wishing she could wave a magic wand and change the past. 'I can't ever make up for the way I behaved, but please believe me when I say I'm truly, truly sorry.'

He didn't say anything, just nodded his head as though he didn't trust himself to speak any more.

'Come on,' he said surprisingly softly, and though he put his arm around her shoulders, she knew it was only to guide her back to the car.

CHAPTER ELEVEN

'MY SON AND I have a lot of catching up to do.'

That was what Andreas had said when they had been driving back from that beauty spot the day he had found out about Theo, and true to his word he had immediately seen to it that they made a start.

Rearranging his work schedule, he had taken a week's emergency leave from his office so that he could be with Theo, and he had certainly gone out of his way over the past week to spend as much time with the little boy as he could.

Theo had been thrilled when Magenta had broken it to him gently that Andreas Visconti was his father—although Andreas had insisted on being there too. As was his right, Magenta had accepted, and she had even been relieved that he had—just as she was pleased that he was so determined to be a hands-on father whenever he could.

What she still couldn't get used to, or help feeling uneasy about, however, was the way he was suddenly wanting a say in all her decisions about Theo—particularly as the little boy was treating him with such adulation, looking up to this new and exciting Daddy as though the man had always been in her life.

'I know you want to be self-sufficient and not dependent upon me in any way, Magenta,' he'd said, the day he had turned up at her flat with the Mini, 'and I'm sorry, but that isn't the way I function. I have a responsibility to you now—if only for my son's sake—so you're going to have to accept this with the good grace with which it's being given.'

There was nothing she could say to that, so she didn't—although she did stand by her guns over the issue of not working for him. It was torture enough having to see him regularly now because of Theo, without subjecting herself to the aching need for him on a daily and more formal basis, when it was all too clear to her that he was never likely to return her love.

She had all but poured her heart out to him that afternoon when she had told him the truth about Theo, and yet he hadn't pursued the subject of her feelings for him any further.

He obviously didn't want to do anything to make his son think that his parents were an item, she realised wretchedly, which could only mean that he had decided they never would be. After all, securing her capitulation when he had only himself to consider was one thing. Finding out that the child of the woman he'd been hell-bent on humiliating was actually his, and not some other man's, must have put a totally different complexion on things altogether.

Consequently on those days when he called round to take her and Theo out she was careful not to give him any indication of the way she felt. She avoided his eyes whenever she felt him looking at her, did her best to hide how the smallest degree of physical contact with him affected her and managed to maintain a cool, emotional distance, although it was agony.

'Relax,' he advised one day, when she was handing over her debit card to pay for something for Theo. He had misunderstood the reason for the way she'd gasped when his strong fingers over hers had stopped her from doing so. 'I know it's an experience you didn't want, having your child's father in the boy's life, but you're going to have to get used to it,' he said quietly, for her alone to hear, and he handed his own card to the cashier.

Taking further control, that week he had secured the riding

lessons for Theo that Magenta had been worried she would have to cancel, ignored her protests and renewed the lease on her flat and, to top it all, charmed her indomitable aunt into giving him one of her home-made blueberry pies.

'How does it feel to suddenly be everybody's favourite person?' Magenta snapped at the end of the week, when they were driving back to her flat after that gesture from her aunt, with Theo asleep in the back of the car.

Andreas laughed deeply under his breath. 'Do I detect some resentment there, Magenta?'

'Of course not,' she answered, adding as casually as she could, 'It's nice that you've been an instant hit with my family.'

But not with her, Andreas thought, conscious of the fact that she didn't really want him in her life. Although that was hardly surprising when she knew as well as he did that his sole intention in employing her had, from the start, been to humiliate her and teach her the lesson he'd felt she deserved. During that week of their working together, however, something else had taken over. Something that ever since had had him waking up feeling that he would go crazy if he couldn't kiss her lovely mouth again and feel her warm, responsive body beneath his.

Noticing the way she was looking over her shoulder at the little boy, with her lips curved in a gentle smile, as he pulled up outside her flat he had to fight the urge to drag her across the car—even with his son in the back—and plunder that luscious mouth until she smiled at *him* like that. Nevertheless, the way she had referred to Theo and Josie a moment ago as *her* family grated, and he had to restrain himself from making any comment and fuelling an already-difficult situation as he carried his sleeping son into the flat.

'As you know, I won't be here for most of next week,' he said, after they had tucked him up in bed, reminding her of the phone conversation he'd had with his colleague earlier in the day. 'I'm doing a tour of the properties in the Lake District and the north-east that I'm going to be taking over from PJ. It *was* scheduled for this week, but in view of more pressing developments...' He didn't need to explain how essential it had been for him to postpone as much as he had been able to in favour of getting to know his boy. 'I'll be gone until Thursday. That's if Lana's managed to book us an afternoon flight—'

'Lana?' she was querying, before he could finish.

'Yes, Lana Barleythorne. You met her at your interview,' he said unnecessarily. 'She'll be coming with me.'

He was about to tell her why, but decided not to, leaving her to speculate as he tried to gauge her reaction. In truth he was wishing that he could leave the adoring Miss Barleythorne securely grounded in the office, but she was becoming a darned good project manager and he was going to need her skills on this country house hotels enterprise—which was why he'd deemed it necessary to have her with him.

Now, though, as Magenta said only, 'Right,' with a dismissive little shrug, he wondered with some annoyance whether he shouldn't take the time to enjoy some of the pleasures that Lana would be more than willing to offer him. At least then, he thought, as he did the sensible thing and left the shabby little flat for the sake of his sanity, he might be able to appreciate a woman as he'd always done—on a purely casual basis—and drive this insane craving for Magenta out of his mind.

Over the next week, although she willed herself not to, Magenta missed Andreas terribly. She didn't know which was worse: hearing from him when he rang sometimes to speak to Theo and make casual conversation with her, or not hearing from him at all. She was getting through each day, she realised, just living for his phone calls, and she berated herself for loving him and for even thinking about him so much when she should have been doing what she had always done until Andreas had come into her life again—and that was channelling all her energies towards her son.

Having agreed to Andreas's request not to pursue the idea of getting another job, at least until after Theo started back to school, Magenta took the little boy out every day—either with her aunt or on her own.

Making the most of the continuing sunshine she took him to the park, or to their local nature reserve, or just to his favourite café, where she bought him an extra thick milkshake as a special treat. She started using the Mini too, which she'd accepted for Theo's benefit. Everything Andreas was doing for them was for Theo's benefit, she reflected painfully, since he'd found out that the boy was his.

At night she read to Theo, as she had done from when he was very small, encouraging him to read to her in turn, keen to develop his interest in books from an early age—which was probably why he was showing such an aptitude for learning now. Some nights they would watch a cartoon, or one of his favourite wildlife DVDs together while he was eating his supper, and then she would tuck him up in bed and tell him a story until his eyelids started to droop and he fell asleep.

Alone then, she would find her thoughts wandering too readily to Andreas—although the idea of him being away for nearly a week with a woman whose interest in him had been patently obvious at that interview was more than her bruised and aching heart could take.

She was glad when the torment was over and the Thursday of that week brought him back.

He had told her that Simon would be picking her and Theo up in the limousine that afternoon, to drive them over to Surrey. He was inviting them both to stay for a long weekend. 'We're going to need to discuss his future,' he'd said, in a way that had made her stomach muscles clench painfully. 'We can't go on without any set course, and it's best that we each know where we stand from the start.'

It was with increasing anxiety, therefore, that late that afternoon Magenta sat browsing through a magazine under the shade of a sun umbrella at the poolside, while Theo paddled in the little inflatable pool that Simon had filled with water. It had been another purchase by Andreas last week, for his son to use at the house in case his parents couldn't be with him in the main pool.

Later, when his flight had been delayed and he'd called to say he wasn't sure whether he was going to be able to make it back by that evening, Magenta showered and changed from her jeans and T-shirt into a simple white sundress as the day was still so warm. After letting Theo watch one of his early evening kiddies' programmes, she decided to put him to bed.

'I want to stay up and wait for Daddy,' the little boy protested sleepily as she was helping him into his pyjamas in the room that the housekeeper had prepared for him next to Magenta's. He was already rubbing his eyes to try and keep them open, but Magenta smiled understandingly.

'I'll send Daddy up to see you as soon as he comes in,' she promised, and was startled to realise how much she sounded like a normal wife and mother, in a normal loving partnership, waiting for her devoted husband to come home.

She knew, though, that Theo would be asleep in seconds after all his excitement that day—riding in the limousine, splashing about in his pool and hitting balls about on the tennis court with her until they had nearly laughed themselves hysterical.

'I don't even know if he'll be coming home tonight,' she whispered, kissing the little boy who looked so much like Andreas with her throat contracting. But already she was saying it to herself.

The sun was throwing its colours over the evening countryside when she stepped out onto the terrace, with dazzling gold already turning to pink by the time she'd crossed the lawn and reached the honeysuckle hedge.

The resident thrush was singing from the uppermost branch of an ancient larch tree, and the air was mellifluous with humming insects and the gentle gurgling of the brook.

She deliberately avoided looking at the lovers' seat. She didn't want to remember what had happened the last time she had sat down on that seat. Nor did she wish to remember what had happened in the house behind her when she had been here last—the torrid passion she had shared with Andreas that had finally shocked her into remembering.

The thrush had stopped singing and the sun was a big red ball through the trees by the time she made up her mind that he wasn't coming home tonight. With an agonised sigh she decided to go back inside—but she'd only made it to the end of the honeysuckle hedge before being brought up fast in her tracks.

'Andreas!' It was more of a gasp than anything else as every cell in her body went into meltdown from his devastating and achingly familiar presence.

English in all but looks and name, he was still wearing the short-sleeved white shirt and sleek grey trousers he'd worn for business that day—although he was tieless now, and his shirt was partially unbuttoned as usual. The perfect tailoring seemed to have moulded itself to every contour of his superb masculinity, and Magenta could only stand and gaze up at him, her lips parted in the sensual paralysis that seemed to have invaded her body.

'I didn't think you'd be out here...'

He too seemed unable to speak fluidly, or like her, to move. He took one stride forward—and Magenta didn't know how it happened but the next second she was in his arms and their hungry mouths were fusing, tasting, devouring each other, while their breathing came hard and impassioned and their faces were illuminated by the crimson glow of the setting sun.

Andreas's lips moved to her neck, her throat, her shoulders, and she was glorying in their ravaging possession, giving herself up to their mutual hunger, to everything she had been wanting, craving, needing, over the past lonely weeks. She didn't care about the past—about yesterday—nor even tomorrow. All she cared about was that they were both here—now—tonight—and nothing in the world could prevent what was going to happen next.

When he drew her urgently down onto the grass beside the lovers' seat she was more than ready for him, helping him as he tugged at her briefs and taking him into her with a cry of pleasure that came from the depths of her soul.

Her climax was swift and sweet, coming with his in a burst of pulsating sensation that was as glorious and spectacular as the sunset. It had all happened so fast that when she turned her head and looked at the red ball again through the trees it was still hanging on the edge of the horizon, like a silent witness to their reckless and unrestrained passion.

'I'm sorry,' Andreas said, breathless. 'I shouldn't have done that.' Already he was getting to his feet. 'I just couldn't stop myself.'

Magenta was breathing as rapidly as he was as she struggled to find her voice. 'Neither could I.'

'Then there's no harm done?' he suggested.

She couldn't look at him as she brushed down the fabric of her crushed dress.

'No.' Why was he saying that? 'Why should there be?' she managed to say casually, though she was hurting inside after having dared for a few moments to imagine that everything might have changed.

'Why, indeed?' He gave her a sort of ruminative half-smile, his eyes appearing dark and reflective, but then he seemed to gather control of himself as he finished adjusting his shirt and trousers. 'So it really doesn't matter?'

How could she tell him that it did? That it mattered very much?

'No.'

'Why?' he asked, in a slightly more abrasive tone. 'Because it's only sex?'

Magenta could scarcely speak now. 'Yes.'

How hard it was to lie!

'In that case you won't be too upset,' he said, plucking one of the honeysuckle flowers, 'if I tell you that...' He hesitated, tossing the delicate creamy flower aside. 'I'm thinking of getting married.'

The earth seemed to freeze on its axis, and with it every stirring leaf and insect.

'No, of course not.' How could she say that and not reveal how much her voice was trembling?

'Honestly?' Was that relief in his eyes? Surprise?

She wanted to say, *No, I'm happy for you.* After all she had had her chance with him a long time ago and she had thrown it right back in his face.

Instead she uttered, 'Wh-who is it? Lana?'

'Lana?' He laughed out loud. 'I'm sure she's very pretty, and has hidden depths that will make some man a very good wife one day,' he remarked, coming away from the flowers, 'but not for me, I'm afraid. No...' He spoke with that hesitation again, as though he was finding it difficult telling her. 'She's a woman I met some time ago.'

'You never mentioned her.'

'No...' He slipped his hands into his trouser pockets, glancing at the dipping sun that was only half visible now above the western horizon. 'The time hasn't been right.'

Involuntarily Magenta nodded, lifting a shaky hand to her dishevelled hair. Somehow, it seemed, since his startling revelation she'd forgotten how to breathe, and after a deep inhalation, she said, 'Wouldn't she be rather upset to think that you...that we've just...?' Unable to say it, she caught the quizzical sidelong glance he sent her way. 'Are you going to tell her?'

She gave a half-shake of her head and felt the throb of an

incipient headache at her temples. Suddenly the last bursts of flame from the fast disappearing sun seemed too glaring, much too painful for her to look at.

'Have you made love with her?' *Dear heaven! Why was she asking him this?* 'I mean recently? Since we…?'

'Yes.'

His answer really did almost take her breath away. Well, what had she expected? she thought, wondering how he could make such amazing love to her when there was another woman—a woman he loved more—in his life. But why was it so surprising that he should have so little respect for her that he could bed her as if it didn't matter and then go off with someone else? He probably still believed that she had done the very same thing to him.

'It does mean,' he said, 'that there will be someone here all the time to help me with Theo when he's here, and you must agree that that will make for a far better situation all round.'

Oh, God! She couldn't bear it! Suddenly her eyes were welling with scalding tears.

'Gosh! This sun's unbearable! It's making my eyes water!' And her voice was thickening with so much emotion that she had to get away.

As she brushed hastily past him, intent only on putting as much distance between them as she could, he was springing after her.

'Magenta!'

'Let me go!'

His hand was like a vice around her wrist. She was crying now, and it was too late for her to run from him, although she kept her face averted to try and delay the moment when he would eventually see.

'Magenta, look at me?'

'Why? Isn't it enough that you had my humiliation once without putting the knife in and twisting it round for one final time?'

'You're crying?' His hand was cupping her face, fingers touching her tears. His brow was furrowing in the gathering dusk.

'So I am!' Her tone was wounded; indignant. 'Are you going to make an issue of that too?'

'I thought you said it was the sun.' Something like amusement coloured his deep voice. 'But lo and behold! *"Tears fall in my heart like the rain..."!*'

Was he mocking her? Ridiculing her with some quotation or other? How could he?

'It isn't funny!'

'No, it damn well isn't!' His tone had changed in an instant, and with it his expression. 'But you'll do anything rather than admit it, won't you?' His chest was puffed out in anger now as he forced her to face him. '*Won't you?*' he rasped, almost shaking her.

'Admit what?' It was a hopeless attempt to maintain her dignity.

'How you feel?'

'How I feel?' She tried to wriggle free but he wouldn't let her. 'You don't *know* how I feel!'

'Don't I?'

'No!'

'Then why are you crying? And why are you shaking so much just from the thought that I might be getting married?'

'I'm not!'

'And why can you never stop yourself when we do this?'

His mouth came down over hers in a kiss that demanded, was almost brutal.

'You've said yourself. It's just sex,' she parried desperately when he released her mouth.

'No, it isn't! Not for me. Not for you. Not for either of us,' he said hoarsely, confounding her, because she couldn't grasp or understand what he was saying. 'But that's beside the point—because you're going to tell me, Magenta!'

'Tell you what?'

'Why you're crying.'

'So you can have your last pound of flesh? Is that it? Is that why you're forcing me to say it? All right, then! I love you!' Her head dropped back and she sagged against him in defeat. 'I love you. So, so much…'

'Then why didn't you tell me before this?'

'You know why.'

She couldn't understand why he was looking and sounding as though all the demons from hell had suddenly been let loose to torment him. The night was drawing in, but even in the encompassing darkness she could make out the anguished lines scoring his face. Why? Magenta wondered. When he should be looking triumphant? When he'd just taken great pains to disclose his intention to marry someone else?

'Because you thought I'd use it against you? To hurt you?'

Wasn't he going to? She couldn't understand the incredulity she heard in his voice.

'Oh, I'll admit I wanted to,' he was saying. 'When you threw away everything I thought we had six years ago. And when you turned up for that interview after pretending—as I thought—not to remember me in that wine bar… Well… To get you in my bed and make you pay through your submission suddenly became the only thing that mattered. My father died the night you left, while we were arguing over you, and I wanted to hold you solely responsible for it.'

She uttered a small groan at this further revelation, and yet there had been a note of self-deprecating futility in his voice.

'It was my fault entirely, but I needed to blame someone else so I blamed you—for everything: what happened to him, what you'd done to me. And I let it fester away inside me for years. When I kissed you in that lift it was to see if you'd respond to me. But as soon as I'd got you here I realised that I'd already bitten off more than I could possibly chew. I wanted to stay immune, to be the one in control this time, but even before that night we made love I'd already discovered I was no more immune to you than I'd been when we were just kids. When I'd found out you'd had that brain haemorrhage…'

His voice trembled as he cupped her face lovingly with both hands. 'Any desire to hurt you went well and truly out of the window. And not because I felt sorry for you…' He shook his head, as though unable to put it into words. 'After we'd made love I wanted you to stay here, because I couldn't imagine letting you out of my life again, but you seemed so determined to go. I knew it was because you believed my only intention was to hurt and humiliate you, and I couldn't seem to convince you that it wasn't. I don't think I really knew myself at the time why I wanted you to stay.' He grimaced. 'Or I wasn't ready to admit it. But then I spent the fortnight after you'd gone wondering why it was driving me so crazy not to have you around. And that day you told me about Theo and all that you had been through after we broke up—I knew.'

It still pole-axed him to think of the terrible struggles and the odds she had faced from which she had come through fighting. Alone. With his baby. And without him.

'I love you, Magenta. I've wanted to tell you so often over the past couple of weeks but you've seemed so distant. So cool.'

'Only because you were!' she exclaimed, trying to take in all that he was telling her. 'But why did you let me think you were marrying someone else?' Pain etched her face as her eyes scoured the shadowy structured lines of his. 'You aren't, are you?' She was still not able to believe that it wasn't true.

'Are you crazy?' He laughed, and now all the earlier anguish in his voice was giving way to pure and simple joy. 'I wasn't absolutely certain that I wasn't kidding myself in believing you might possibly be in love with me. And, forgive me, my darling, for being so devious—and too proud to face rejection if I really had been kidding myself—but it was the only way I could think of finding out.'

'You…!' She thumped him playfully, her eyes brimming with happiness, and through a blur of tears she saw the first sliver of a crescent moon rising in the night sky.

'Surely you must have realised that I was referring to you?'

Magenta shook her head, but then started to see how she might have if she'd dared to let herself believe it.

'Marry me.'

It was a request he had made of her a long time ago, but now she responded to his husky demand with a heart that was almost too full to contain.

'You try and stop me,' she warned him, the second before his face blanked out the moon.

An owl hooted somewhere in the woods across the brook, but the night breezes did nothing to cool their rising passion, and a small thrill ran through Magenta when Andreas lifted his head, just before things got too far out of hand again, to murmur excitingly, 'No. In bed this time.'

EPILOGUE

THEIR WEDDING IN the little register office yesterday had gone well, Magenta reflected, lounging in the big bed overlooking the softly illuminated Bermudian beach, waiting for her husband to join her. She had worn a short white Sixties-style smock dress that had complemented the small flowers in her hair while still keeping from everyone but the few people closest to her the wonderful secret of her three-month pregnancy.

Theo had been a page, standing proudly and with amazing solemnity behind his parents in a little dark suit and bowtie, while Aunt Josie had dabbed at her eyes from under a large brown hat through most of the service, proclaiming afterwards that something—dust or an eyelash—must have got in.

Jeanette James had flown over from Portugal, looking prettier and happier than Magenta had seen her look in years, and she knew it was all to do with the gentle silver-haired man at her side. Things had been awkward between her mother and Andreas when her mother had first arrived two days ago, and she had declined their offer of hospitality in favour of staying in a hotel. But standing there yesterday outside the register office, in a stylish green suit, with her brown hair beautifully cut and highlighted, the woman had genuinely wished them well, and had even reached up to kiss Andreas before being drawn into Aunt Josie's welcoming arms.

Now, as her husband came through from the *en suite* bathroom wearing nothing but a striped silk robe, Magenta's heart gave a little leap, as it always did when she saw him.

'Are you sure you didn't mind leaving Theo behind?' Andreas asked, as he slid in next to her under the light coverlet. 'I know he's ultra-independent, but are you sure he's not likely to fret?'

'With Aunt Josie moving in this week and a new pony to keep him occupied? Hardly!' Magenta laughed, knowing that she was the one more likely to do any fretting while they were parted from their exuberant five-year old. 'And anyway it's only for six days, until they fly over to meet us in Disneyland.'

Satisfied that she was happy, Andreas ran a tender hand down her cheek before reaching round for something under his pillow.

'My Byron!' she exclaimed as he handed her the familiar little book with its velvety green suede cover. 'You've had it repaired!'

And so expertly that no one would ever guess that it had once been damaged.

'We've rebuilt so much. Put everything right between us,' Andreas said. 'It would have been remiss of me not to have included this as well.'

Reclining there in a sheath of white lace and satin, Magenta ran treasuring fingers over the book's soft cover. He could have thrown it away six years ago, she thought. She remembered him telling her once that he almost had. But his grandmother had found it and put it away for him for when he returned from America, so she guessed she had Maria Visconti to thank for that.

'There are some lines from that favourite poem of mine,' she told him softly as they drifted to the forefront of her mind. 'And somehow I couldn't say anything better to you tonight to express exactly how I feel. "From the wreck of the past, which hath perish'd",' she quoted, '"Thus much I at least may recall…"'

A silencing thumb brushed gently over her lips as he finished the verse for her. "'It hath taught me that what I most cherish'd, Deserved to be dearest of all.'"

Her eyes filled with tears, because he was so very dear and he had done so much. For her and for Theo. For her great-aunt. But most of all because he had given her back his love when she might so easily have lost it for ever.

'My Magi...'

Her heart missed a beat as he breathed the name only he'd ever used against the thick shining tumble of her hair.

'I always was,' she whispered. 'Even when you thought I'd left you, I hadn't.' She put a hand to her chest. 'Not here inside.'

As he took the book from her and laid it on the bedside cabinet she slid down and looked up at the fan circulating on the ceiling in wild anticipation of yet another glorious night ahead. It was just one in a long line of glorious nights they had spent already, since he had proposed to her by the lovers' seat three months ago, and Magenta knew it was only the beginning of a lifetime of glorious nights and days ahead that they would share together.

At some stage in the future, she thought absently, she might put her business skills to use again, but for the foreseeable future she was looking forward simply to being a wife and mother.

'You know, from what I've heard Lord Byron was really quite irresistible to women,' she murmured as Andreas switched off the bedside lamp. 'I suppose it comes from knowing the female sex inside out.' Then, with definite teasing in her voice, she added, 'A pity a girl can't stumble upon that type of man today, really...'

And then she let out a shriek as Andreas pulled her under him and proceeded to show her that she could.

* * * * *

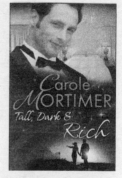

Come home this Christmas to Fiona Harper

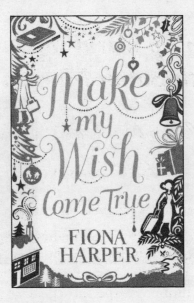

From the author of *Kiss Me Under the Mistletoe* comes a Christmas tale of family and fun. Two sisters are ready to swap their Christmases—the busy super-mum, Juliet, getting the chance to escape it all on an exotic Christmas getaway, whilst her glamorous work-obsessed sister, Gemma, is plunged headfirst into the family Christmas she always thought she'd hate.

www.millsandboon.co.uk

1113/MB442

Wrap up warm this winter with Sarah Morgan...

Sleigh Bells in the Snow

Kayla Green loves business and hates Christmas.

So when Jackson O'Neil invites her to Snow Crystal Resort to discuss their business proposal... the last thing she's expecting is to stay for Christmas dinner. As the snowflakes continue to fall, will the woman who doesn't believe in the magic of Christmas finally fall under its spell...?

4th October

www.millsandboon.co.uk/sarahmorgan

She's loved and lost — will she ever learn to open her heart again?

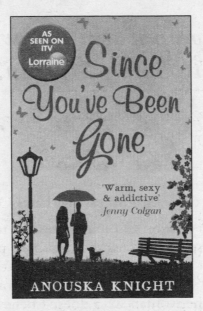

From the winner of ITV Lorraine's Racy Reads, Anouska Knight, comes a heart-warming tale of love, loss and confectionery.

'The perfect summer read — warm, sexy and addictive!'
—Jenny Colgan

For exclusive content visit:
www.millsandboon.co.uk/anouskaknight